DO208476

She didn't set out t...

It was just…a kiss seemed a way to halt him in his tracks.

All she did was frame his face in her hands and press her lips against his for a couple of seconds. That was all it took for Maguire to go from manic-energy machine to statue still.

With that first contact, her lips seemed to instantly recognize that Maguire was nothing like any man she'd ever known.

She'd felt so trapped these past two months, caged so tightly she couldn't seem to free herself. Maguire had inserted himself in the role of her white knight—more like her kidnapper—but that wasn't the man she found herself kissing.

It wasn't a hero who kissed her back.

It was a man.

Dear Reader,

I was thinking about my daughter when I wrote this book. She came out of the womb knowing how to handle men—she had her father doing anything she wanted before she could even talk. Of course she's beautiful… and kind…so that was part of the picture.

The story idea came from that premise…. The hero initially thinks he's handling the heroine (of course). He comes into her life when she's in trouble, pitches in like the true hero he is. (He was *so* fun to write!) But even though he didn't know it—and probably still doesn't—my heroine was really doing all the handling.

He rescues her…but she rescues him right back.

I hope you like the story! And please feel to write me, either through my website, www.jennifergreene.com, or the Facebook page for "Jennifer Greene Author."

Jennifer Greene

THE BILLIONAIRE'S HANDLER

JENNIFER GREENE

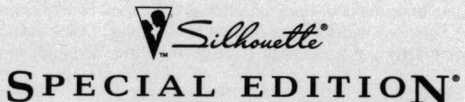

SPECIAL EDITION®

Published by Silhouette Books

America's Publisher of Contemporary Romance

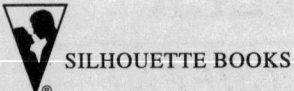 **SILHOUETTE BOOKS**

ISBN-13: 978-0-373-65563-2

Recycling programs for this product may not exist in your area.

THE BILLIONAIRE'S HANDLER

Copyright © 2010 by Alison Hart

Visit Silhouette Books at www.eHarlequin.com

Printed in U.S.A.

JENNIFER GREENE

lives near Lake Michigan with her husband and an assorted menagerie of pets. Michigan State University has honored her as an outstanding woman graduate for her work with women on campus.

Jennifer has written more than seventy love stories, for which she has won numerous awards, including four RITA® Awards from the Romance Writers of America and both their Hall of Fame and Lifetime Achievement Awards.

You're welcome to contact Jennifer through her website at www.jennifergreene.com.

To Jennifer Jeanne
You have the biggest heart of anyone I know
Love you.

Prologue

Maguire climbed aboard, wasting no time before kicking off his shoes and sinking into the white leather couch. Maybe he was stuck suffering through a Puccini opera tonight, but there were advantages to being the lone traveler on a private jet. Not only did he own the escape vehicle—which was mighty convenient—but on the long-hour flight to New York, he could bank a serious snooze.

That was the plan.

But he closed his eyes, expecting to hear the door close and the engines start up. Instead, he heard a kid's breathless voice, yelling all the way from the tarmac.

"Mr. Cochran? Mr. Cochran!"

The boy wore a courier uniform, and bounded into the cabin with a flushed face and a self-important air.

"I was told to deliver this to you immediately, sir."

"Thank you." Maguire tipped him and sent him on his way. The pilot had already stepped out of the cockpit to see if there was a problem. Maguire asked him to hold up for two shakes until he had a chance to find out what was so critical in the ordinary manila envelope.

The return address warned him, but the picture that spilled out brought an immediate scowl to his forehead.

He'd seen the photo before. The young woman was sitting on a carpet with a half-dozen children. The kids all appeared to be disabled in different ways. They were clapping hands with her, playing some kind of game or song. She was sitting on her knees, just like the kids, her pale hair wisping around her cheeks, her eyes full of laughter. Everything about her looked as fragile as powder.

"The situation has deteriorated," was the opening line in the report from his investigator.

Maguire read on. Some of it, he already knew. The job she loved was in jeopardy. Her place was constantly hounded by strangers. She'd tried a change in phones, which was like plugging a finger in a dike. Then she'd tried security, but what she knew about security measures wouldn't fill a thimble. A second photo showed an exhausted woman with shadowed eyes, who looked as if she'd been eating a nonstop diet of nerves and stress.

The break-in was the recent development.

"The police are looking into it," his investigator reported, "but this could be the straw that broke the camel's back. Last night her brother visited her. He called an ambulance. At this time, I've been unable to substantiate what the medical problem is."

Maguire put down the envelope, his mind spinning a hundred miles an hour. None of this should have anything to do with him. He hadn't caused the crisis, didn't even know the damn woman.

Even though his father had died, it seemed Maguire was still stuck cleaning up the man's messes.

"Sir?" The pilot hovered in the cockpit doorway, waiting for instructions.

"See how fast you can change flight plans. We're canceling the New York trip. I need to fly into South Bend, Indiana."

He put a dozen things in motion within minutes, as if he'd been prepared for this contingency for some time—which, of course, he had. He'd known this could happen. Known he might have to become involved.

Sometimes there was a problem that only a billionaire could handle. The irony was that money had nothing to do with it.

Chapter One

When Carolina Daniels opened her eyes, she seemed to have dropped into someone else's life.

Nothing in her vision was familiar.

The blue blanket comfortably snuggled under her chin wasn't hers. The pillow under her head was flat instead of poofy and the serene blue walls and contemporary decor had nothing in common with her bedroom. The room wasn't just tidy; there wasn't a single mess in sight—no open books, no shoes, no sweaters draping chairs, no half-opened bag of Oreos by the bed.

The lack of Oreos was proof positive. Either someone had given her a character transplant, or she really was living someone else's life.

That thought almost struck her as funny, except that her mind was groggier than glue. Someone had given her some heavy-duty drugs, judging from her woozy mind. Still, there seemed no reason to be afraid, exactly. The room was peaceful, silent. Sleeping on a comfortable bed, cuddled in a warm blanket, hardly portended a dangerous situation. It was just that her mind was so murky she really couldn't grasp where she was or why.

But then she spotted the man. Her heart abruptly hiccuped. A major hiccup. A major, serious hiccup.

The crazy dream had taken an immediate dramatic turn, but whether it was evolving into an erotic fantasy or a nightmare, she couldn't tell. At least not yet. She tried closing her eyes. Reopening them.

The stranger was still there, prowling the perimeter of the room like a caged-up lion, a cell phone pressed to his ear. Carolina didn't know him. He wore a dark gray suit, of a cut and fabric that looked European. A stark white shirt and charcoal striped tie were both yanked loose at the throat. A guy could go to the opera in Paris wearing clothes that expensive and distinctive.

But it wasn't his clothes that had her heart suddenly pounding like a trapped bird's. It was him. Something about him.

Everything about him.

Still talking on his cell phone, he turned on his heel, about to face her way. Instinctively she closed her eyes so he wouldn't realize she was awake, but her mind had already cataloged his features.

Only pale daylight seeped through the lone window, just enough to reveal his face, his stature. She guessed he was a few years older than her twenty-eight, but not many, maybe five or six. Although he was dressed for a formal night out, his blond hair looked hand shoveled, his chin peppered with whiskers, his sharp blue eyes shadowed with weariness. He was tall. Of course, everyone was annoyingly tall compared to Carolina's five-four…but he was *really* tall. Easily a couple inches over six feet. He was built long, lean and mean, with shoulders wide enough to fill a doorway.

He wasn't a next-door-neighbor type. He was more the kind of someone who ran things. Big things. Someone who made people jump and events happen. Energy and power charged the air around him, in the way he stalked about, the way his muscles bunched, the way his jaw squared off as he spoke into the phone. Maybe he was an extraordinarily compelling hunk…but she sure wouldn't want to be on the wrong side of an argument with him.

But those were just more reasons why she wouldn't, didn't, couldn't know him. Her circle of people—from her fellow special ed teachers to family to all her neighbors in the new South Bend condo complex—just never crossed paths with anyone like this man.

Her muzzy mind processed more information. The monitors and equipment off to her right suggested she was in a hospital, even if the silk-blue walls and couch and flat-screen TV hardly resembled standard hospital decor. Again, she tried to recall why she was here, how she'd gotten here, but it was as if there was a door in her mind. On one side of the door was something huge and upsetting and exhausting, something so overwhelming that she couldn't gather the strength to force that door open.

Her arms were wrapped around her knees, her knees tucked to her chin. She remembered curling up this way when she was a little girl in the dark, trying to hide, to make herself invisible so the alligators under the bed couldn't find her.

But she wasn't a little girl, and there were no alligators now. Just the strange man who seemed to have popped into her life with no more logic than a dream. He suddenly spun around, lasered a compelling stare in her direction again—and caught her eyes open.

Immediately he snapped the cell phone shut and strode straight toward her. His mouth opened, as if he was furiously barking out orders to people unseen, people behind him, but she couldn't hear what he was saying.

Bits and pieces of reality started seeping into her mind. Nothing about him. But about that crisis moment when she suddenly lost her hearing.

The last weeks all came back in a blotchy rush. The stunned joy and shock when she was told about the fabulous inheritance. The disbelief. The thrill. The racing around her apartment like a mad thing, screaming at the top of her lungs, calling everyone she knew. Checking back twice with the lawyer to make sure it was real.

But when that giant check arrived, so did repercussions that she'd never anticipated, and had no possible way to be prepared for.

Two days ago? Three? She remembered her brother's face when he'd found her. Gregg looked so scared. She'd been locked in her bedroom, hands over her ears, wrapped in an old wool stadium blanket in the corner. No one could reach her, she'd thought. She'd pulled out the landline, drowned the cell phone in the tub. And anyway, she couldn't hear anymore.

Hysterical deafness, the doctor had called it. There was nothing medically wrong with her ears, with her hearing. The doctor never specifically labeled her a head case, but Carolina had always been one to call a cigar a cigar. She'd caved like a ninny. It was embarrassing and mortifying—but being mad at herself didn't seem to bring her hearing back.

Still. None of those events explained how she'd

gotten in this specific hospital room, or who the powerful sexy stranger was…much less what he was doing anywhere near her life.

Maguire had debated between the Lear 35A or the Gulfstream III, but by late afternoon, he was pleased that he'd opted for the Gulfstream. It was the older jet, not as fancy as the Lear, but the full-size divan in back made the most comfortable possible bed for Carolina.

By then they'd passed the rainy Great Plains, hit a burst of late-afternoon sun and the first view of the mountains. Any other time, Maguire would have enjoyed the flight. Now, though, he was too restless to settle down, and kept getting up to check on the slight, blond woman in back.

Carolina didn't need him keeping vigil. Every time he checked, she was sleeping like a stone. He just couldn't seem to stop looking at her.

Spiriting her away—Maguire didn't like the "kidnapping" term—had been challenging, but not impossible. Money, of course, always effectively eliminated problems. He just normally did nothing impulsively. He'd been monitoring Carolina's life for the last two months, but he never expected she would ever have to know that—much less that he'd have to suddenly and completely step in.

It's not as if he suddenly wanted this woman in his life.

He'd had absolutely no choice.

"Mr. Cochran?"

Maguire glanced up at the pilot's voice. "Problem?"

"A little turbulence coming. I'd prefer you strap in."

Right. Maguire had flown too often with Henry to believe "turbulence" was the issue. Henry was worried about their passenger, and even more worried about what his employer was up to this time.

"I'll be there in a minute," he said, yet still he lingered by Carolina.

He'd covered Carolina earlier with a silk sheet and lightweight blanket. She hadn't stirred in the hours since he'd lifted her from the stretcher on the tarmac and carried her aboard.

He hadn't been the one to sedate her, was totally against drugging her at all, and he'd had a rousing argument with the hospital doctor about…well, just about everything. Her medicines. Her treatment. What she needed. That Maguire had no business taking her off someplace without medical permission or involvement. All that blah blah blah.

But that was water over the dam at this point. He checked the straps, making sure she couldn't fall or be thrown, and then redraped the blanket up to her chin. She kept kicking off the cover. He didn't want her exposed to drafts.

That simplest, basic contact—his knuckles to her bare throat, nothing intimate about it in any way— sent a sharp streak of desire straight to his groin. The darned woman. There was absolutely nothing to explain that scissor stab of sexual awareness.

She was as ordinary as peaches and cream. Her features were more fun than attractive—a miniature ski jump for a nose, bitsy cheekbones, a mouth almost too small to kiss. Her hair was butter yellow, mixed with a little pale wheat, might be shoulder length—it was hard to tell; it was such a curly mess. He doubted the whole package could weigh a hundred and ten pounds, and he should know, since he'd carried her up the plane's steps. No butt or boobs that he'd noticed.

He'd caught an unexpected glimpse of her bare feet, though. The toenails were painted a wild purple—a startling surprise.

Except for those wild toenails, she looked beyond vulnerable. Frail. As if a slap would beat her down.

Maguire's father hadn't slapped her. At his death, Gerald Cochran had left her fifteen million dollars. What should have been an incredible gift had turned into an incredible burden—and there was precisely the problem. The doctors didn't get it. Lawyers certainly didn't get it. No one in Carolina's hard-working, middle-class family had any prayer of getting it.

That money could destroy her. Maguire knew it too well. In less than two months, it almost had.

"Mr. Cochran."

Henry again. Maguire stood, catwalked up the aisle, past the leather seats and galley to the cockpit, and then strapped himself into the copilot's chair.

He'd hired Henry four years ago. Henry was barely thirty, but he had an old man's face, bassett-hound eyes and forehead wrinkles of worry that were already set in. Maguire always figured Henry came out of the womb an old soul, probably never had a childhood, and for damn sure never stepped on a crack in the sidewalk. But those weren't bad character traits for a pilot and man Friday. Henry had turned into one of the few people Maguire could trust.

"Everything on track?" Maguire asked easily.

"Should be landing by eight. Washington time, of course. Weather patterns look good." Henry lived for flying, yet his expression was as somber as mud.

"But." Maguire knew there was one coming.

Henry shot him a darting glance. "Even for you, sir, this is a little unusual."

"Yeah. I know."

"I'm not questioning you. You know that. It's just that this is so..."

"Unusual," Maguire supplied, when it was obvious

Henry couldn't think of another word to put out there.

"Yes. The lady there…" Henry shook his head. "I just don't quite understand how we're going to communicate with her if she can't hear."

"Beats me. We'll figure something out."

"You don't think it's slightly, say, illegal. To just take her out of that place without her permission?"

"She was having a breakdown, Henry. Because of what my father did. There was no conventional way to make this right. There's no one in her regular life who has a clue what she's trying to cope with. You think I should have walked away?"

"I wouldn't presume to say, sir."

"Well, I didn't have that option. I couldn't walk away. There was no one else who could make this right. This upended my life, too, you know, not just hers." He sighed. "Try to relax, Henry. If I get taken off to prison, I'll make sure you're not implicated."

"That wasn't my concern, sir."

"Once you get a serious night's rest, I want you to fly back to South Bend. I have a list of things you need to do. We're going to set up a communication base so her friends and family have an email address for her, a cell phone just for those communications. I'll deal personally with any and all lawyers. But her place is going to need some maintenance. She'll be with me for several weeks—"

"Several *weeks?*" Harry tugged at his button-down collar.

"Maximum. I'm hoping no more than two weeks, but we could have to extend it to three. Which is why I need you to get back to her place as soon as you've rested up from this flight. Nothing huge to do, just details. See if she has plants to water, empty her fridge of perishables. Call me with a list of personal items in her medicine cabinet, cosmetics, medicines, that kind of thing. Put her heating at a nominal temperature—sixty. Like that."

"No problem."

"I don't know what mail she'll have come in. If there are bills, I want you to pick them up, route them to me. Personal mail, forward. Catalogs or junk, just heap up. This is too much to be telling you off the cuff. I'll give you a list when you're ready."

"You don't need me at the lodge with you?"

"I could. But when she wakes up, first thing she's going to freak about is all the personal life she's left hanging. So we have to take care of that, number one. Beyond those obvious life details, I won't know more than that until she wakes up and starts talking."

"Sir?"

"Henry. Quit doing that careful 'sir' thing. Whatever's bothering you, just get it off your chest before you drive me nuts."

"Yes, sir. What if she wakes up and wants to go home? What if she doesn't want to stay with you?"

"Henry."

"Yes, sir?"

"Of course she won't want to stay with me. She doesn't know me from Adam. But it's my problem to build her trust. To make this work. Not yours."

"Yes, sir."

Maguire sighed. "What's the 'but' now, Henry?"

"It's just….she's young. And very, well, pretty. Very pretty."

"Henry."

"Yes, sir?"

"Have I ever struck you as the kind of man who'd take advantage of a wounded woman?"

"No, sir."

"Have you noticed that I have any lack of attractive women in my life?"

"No, sir."

"And here's the punch line, Henry. I kidnapped her. That means I have the power over the situation. And that means there's no way I'd touch a hair on her head. Got it?"

"Yes, sir."

"If I were burning in hell, Henry. If she begged me. If she were my last chance to have sex in my entire life. Some things are plain wrong, and the line here is crystal clear. While she's under my care, she couldn't be safer."

"Got it, sir."

"Now, are there any more questions, or can I go back and catch an hour of shut-eye?"

"Absolutely no questions, sir."

About every three months or so, Henry revealed a sense of humor. Otherwise it was like having an old-fashioned aunt around, always underfoot, worrying whether he had an umbrella in the rain, whether he'd eaten, whether he was hot or cold or tired. Damn good employee. But exhausting sometimes.

Maguire headed back, grabbed a blanket from an overhead bin and dropped into the oversize lounge chair closest to her. He considered turning on the tube, or switching on his computer, or opening his briefcase. Instead, he found himself staring at Carolina again.

Everything about her was soft. Skin. Hair. Mouth. There wasn't a single hint of toughness in her.

He could well believe she'd risked her life to save his little brother, even though Tommy was a relative stranger to her. He could well believe she wouldn't think, before leaping in, to help someone else.

He couldn't imagine her being tough enough, re-silient enough, to handle the pressure that had been heaped on her in the last two months. She'd never had the training for it, the upbringing that could have prepared her.

His father, so typically, had impulsively left her a gift that was supposed to be generous and wonderful. It would never have occurred to Gerald that he'd thrown a young woman into the deep end with no life raft in sight.

Maguire had to be the life raft.

There was no one else.

And that meant exactly what he'd told Henry. It didn't matter, about her soft skin, or that silky blond hair. It didn't matter that those small, perfect lips challenged a man to want to take them, to mold them, to see exactly what kind of passion might be awakened there. She was a sweet woman. A giver. Those were the facts Maguire already knew.

But whether there was more under that surface, he had to find out. Without touching her. Without harming her in any way.

No matter what it cost him.

Chapter Two

Carolina opened sleepy eyes and abruptly frowned. You'd think she had a wild love life, considering how many strange beds she'd woken up in lately.

Waking up in strange beds was kind of interesting, but waking up feeling drunk-drugged was getting mighty old.

Memories from the last two days came back to her in patches. She remembered her mysterious stranger having a fight with her doctor in the hospital—she couldn't hear it—but remembered them both shaking their heads, stomping around, in each other's faces.

Then…she had no recollection of leaving the hospital, but of waking up on an ultra-fancy private jet on a cushy leather couch. Her kidnapper showed up from time to time. She remembered his hand on her cheek, remembered his finger brushing her hair. Then a landing in a tiny private airport in the dark. At some point there'd been soup. Wild rice. Chicken with basil and cilantro. Incredible cilantro. Then an omelet. Or maybe she'd had the omelet before? And wasn't there another man there? Kind of a little guy, youngish, with thin hair and old-man worried eyes.

The whole thing was so darned blurry. It seemed as if she'd slept for days on days, so how could she still feel so exhausted?

Yet her pulse rate eased as she started looking around. The window view to her right was the stuff of soul smiles. She was definitely nowhere near home. South Bend had no mountains, much less such gorgeous sharp peaks scarfed with snow. At home, the hardwoods would all be reds and golds by this time in October, but not this dramatic mix of huge, droopy pines and sassy yellow aspens.

And then there was the bedroom. Granted, her own place was on the slightly untamed side—all right, all right, she was downright messy. But by any criteria, this one was a gasper.

A copper bed of coals crackled in the corner fireplace. Past a white marble hearth was an Oriental rug, thicker than a mattress, colors in a swirl of black and creams and corals and mustards. The same smoky mustard matched the silk blanket covering her, the muted hue of the walls, and the mustard leather couch in front of the giant window.

And that was when she noticed him again.

Her kidnapper.

He was sitting on the couch, facing the mountains, not her. His fingers were crossed behind his neck. Her attention latched on to what little of him she could see—the tousled head of blond hair, straight and thick. The clipped-short fingernails. He wasn't wearing formal attire this time, but exactly the opposite. The sleeves of his sweatshirt were yanked up, frayed at the cuffs near his elbows. Hair sprinkled his forearms. Not a caveman amount. But enough.

He was such a total guy in every way.

Carolina waited a heartbeat for terror to kick in. He'd spirited her away against her choice or will; he was a strong, virile man, and she had no clue what he wanted from her. Obviously she should be afraid. Not just afraid, but panicked. Terrified.

Instead…

Her pulse bucked. But not with fear. At least not exactly. Even when, as if sensing she was awake, he suddenly whipped his head around and found her gaze on him.

He was up in a flash, crossing the room, but he lifted his hands in a universal gesture indicating,

"Take it easy, take it easy." He bent down, reached for a lipstick-red netbook and carried it toward her.

The minicomputer was already set to word processing, already had words on it.

"I'm Maguire," the first line read. And then, "You can speak, but I know you can't hear. So this is how I can communicate with you. Okay?"

After she read it, she looked up. He was, of course, kidding. Nothing was okay. Still, he plopped at the foot of her bed and started typing, then handed her the netbook again.

"You don't get to grade me on typos. Or speed." He looked up at her again, as if expecting her to reply.

Carolina blinked at him. Alice in Wonderland couldn't have been this bewildered. A strange man was sitting on her bed, in a place where he'd kidnapped her—and seemed to think she'd be in the mood to make jokes.

"Detention for bad spelling," she said firmly. She couldn't hear her own voice, but apparently he did, because he winced, and grabbed the netbook again.

"Okay. Be tough then. But just so you know. I've got the chocolate." He looked up.

So did she, after reading the last words. "You think I can be bought?"

He typed, "Can you?"

She sucked in a breath. The moment of light teasing was fun—but obviously crazy. She turned serious. "I need to know what's going on here. Right now."

His face changed expression. The easy, lazy rascal disappeared. The tough, take-charge guy returned. He typed for a while, then turned the machine around again.

"You're going to get your hearing back. That's part of why you're here. To give you a place to heal, a place with absolutely no stress."

She read that. Looked straight into his eyes. "You know this how? Are you a doctor? Some other kind of health professional? How do you know anything about me?"

He typed for another few minutes. She saw his lips frame a swearword. Then a more volatile swearword. He was quite familiar with the delete button, she noticed, but finally he turned the netbook around again. He really couldn't spell worth beans.

"The big questions, we'll deal with later. Let's just start with first things first—the information you need to know right away. You're safe. Your family and neighbors know you're safe. Your lawyer knows that he can reach you through me. There's nothing you need to worry about—no bills or appointments left hanging. That's all been taken care of."

She read. Looked back at him. This time she had nothing to say. His comments were too audacious. Too impossible.

He grabbed the netbook again, typed fast. "Don't look like that. All upset. It's coming back to you, isn't it? What was happening to you? Your losing your hearing, your brother afraid you were having a breakdown?"

She read that and said nothing. She couldn't. Her life—her real life—suddenly roller-coastered back into mental focus for her, faster than she could stop it. And suddenly there was a lump in her throat the size of a gorilla. Even though she'd slept endlessly for at least the last couple days, she suddenly wanted to curl into a ball again. Close her eyes. She couldn't let it loose again. The anxiety. It was waiting to lunge at her like a rabid dog, scramble with her head, leech all her joy of life again.

A long strong hand covered hers. *"No,"* he said, as if he thought she could hear. And then he brusquely grabbed the netbook again.

"This is the deal, Carolina. On the ottoman, there's a tray with all kinds of breakfast foods. The bathroom's through that far door, if you don't remember. It's already equipped with the basics, and if there's anything else you need, just ask. After that, you can go back to sleep if you want…or come on downstairs, explore the place. Inside, outside, wherever you want to be. There's an office downstairs, with shelves full of books, if you're in the mood to read."

He turned the netbook around. She read that,

slowly nodded. His straight "information" posts were easier to handle.

He raised a finger, took the netbook back. "In return, I need you to make out two lists for me. Sometime today, if you can."

"What kind of lists?" she asked warily.

"One—a list of foods. I need to know if you're allergic to any foods, or if there are any foods you really don't like. I'd like to know your favorites, too. You could make a list like that for me, couldn't you?"

He turned the minicomputer around, let her read the message, but she didn't waste time answering the rhetorical question. And he was already typing again.

"Then, I need you to make out a longer list. We'll call it a dream list. I want you to close your eyes. Think about things you always wanted to see, places you always wanted to explore or visit. Things you always wanted to do that you never had a chance to. Dreams you had as a kid even, that you knew were impractical and unlikely, but you still dreamed 'em. Got it?"

She read the post. Frowned. Some of it took deciphering. "Why?" she asked him.

He typed for a moment longer, but all the post said was, "I can't keep typing. This is killing me. So that's it for now—you have breakfast, check out the shower and come down whenever you're ready. And after you give me those lists, I'll give you more information. Okay?"

She read that, said flat out, "No, it's not okay."

But all she got from him was a quiet smile and a shrug. And then he simply left, making a point of closing the door behind him.

She stayed motionless for several seconds, unsure if he'd return. But when the door stayed closed, she pushed aside the covers and got up. Her head immediately swam….but then cleared. Whatever drugs she'd been taking or given, she could tell they weren't as thick in her system. She was just darned weak.

She checked the domed tray on the round-cushioned ottoman. Found a crystal pitcher with juice, a carafe of coffee, sterling silverware, white linen, covered plates with fruit and an omelet and sides. The elegance of the tray made her pause.

Especially after the last two months, she'd become hypersensitive about money. Any normal person would instinctively assume a kidnapper wanted money, yet that fear never crossed her mind with Maguire. All the evidence indicated he had heaps and heaps of money of his own. The standard criminal hardly traveled via private luxury jet, did he? Or served breakfast with sterling and crystal. Or stashed his victims in a mountain lodge that was gorgeous in every way.

But if he didn't want money, why on earth *had* he kidnapped her?

The mysteries kept mounting.

She walked into the bathroom, found another room to die for.

Every detail was elegant and lavishly comfortable—a copper sink, a tub the size of a wading pool, marble tiles in creams and clays and browns. A flat screen above the tub had menus for a choice of scenic pictures or movies. A swivel door revealing a spa's expansive choice of scrubs and soaps and moisturizers.

She filled the tub and sank in. A hand hose enabled her to shampoo, rinse off, and then just use the pulse spray on tired muscles. A kidnappee should not be feeling safe, she kept telling herself...yet it was just there. The pure sensation of feeling clean, safe, warm.

The things she feared in her real life were far worse than anything she could fear from this stranger. For all the sleep she'd had, there'd been no moments of feeling free from anxiety or pressure.

Yet that crazy moment of safety and peace—of course—couldn't last. Bit by bit, she noticed sudden, jolting details in her surroundings. The first was as simple as the scent of the shampoo she'd just used— she knew it. It was a specific brand to volumize thin hair. *Her* specific choice of brand.

The wonderful, rich almond soap she'd used was exactly the same as the kind she used at home. She glanced at the basket on the marble counter, overflowing with the usual bathroom survival products, from deodorant to toothpaste, manicure tools to toothbrush. Each item was still packaged, new. But they were all her own choice of brands, the same products she bought.

An odd shiver chased up her spine. She wasn't sure whether she should feel cosseted...or controlled.

There were too many products that were the same as the ones she was accustomed to using to be coincidental. Someone had gone to a lot of trouble to know personal things about her, her daily life. And yeah, it had to be the man downstairs. Maguire.

But why?

Belatedly she spotted a robe hung on the bathroom door—Oriental silk, red and black, long, with a thin, slippery sash. The robe definitely wasn't hers, which happened to be pink and old and sexless. Right then, she was happy to put on anything different from the hospital scrubs she'd been wearing.

She dried her hair, brushed her teeth, then wrapped the robe snugly around her before risking opening the door. There was no one in sight. The hallway revealed two closed doors on the other side, which she assumed led to other bedrooms.

At the end of the hall was an open staircase, leading

to a massive downstairs area. It was a lot to take in, in a single visual gulp. A round fireplace dominated the center of the room. Furnishings splashed around that—couches, giant chairs, an oak table polished to the gleam of glass. Floor-to-ceiling windows showed mountain views on all sides, as if the house had fallen from the sky and had been plunked down in the middle of rugged, wild hills.

The place was breathtaking, yet Carolina wrapped her arms around her chest as she tiptoed downstairs. As luxurious and unique as the lodge was, it was also—for her—bizarre.

She was happy to escape the cage her life had turned into, but that still didn't remotely make this situation right. She'd been rested, fed, cleaned up, but now she needed serious answers. A frame for this picture that someone had put her in.

She saw no sign of Maguire. But once she reached the last stair, she realized there was another wing of rooms off to the east. He'd mentioned there was an office or library with books somewhere, but she figured she'd explore that direction later.

For now, the open downstairs captured her attention. Her bare feet sank into thick, soft green carpet. Morning sunlight flushed the room with light. A squirrel scampered along a door ledge. A bevy of goofy-looking quail pecked in the yard, making her smile. It wasn't as if the craziness in her life had disappeared, only that she'd almost forgotten what it was like to have simple moments, enjoying life and sunlight and the easy pleasure of natural things like watching a silly squirrel.

But then a photo snared her attention. Two pictures were framed on the lamp table, but only one of them instantly riveted her attention. She bent down to get a better look.

The small child in the photo was barely a toddler. He was outside—the same yard Carolina could see from the window—running in his pajamas, giggling, joy in his big eyes, his face. Someone was chasing him, causing all the laughter, the fun. The camera had just captured that moment, of a delightfully happy boy with taffy hair and pudgy fingers and unrestrained glee.

Carolina picked up the photograph with trembling fingers.

She knew the child. Tommy. It had to be Tommy.

Her eyes welled with tears. She couldn't seem to help making a keening sound…and then realized, for the first time in ages, she'd not only made that helpless sound of affection and sorrow…

But she'd heard it. Heard her own voice.

Her hearing had finally returned.

Although Maguire never heard her walking around, some sixth sense triggered an awareness that

Carolina had come downstairs. He severed the phone call and crossed the office to the door.

There she was, in the living area. Her hair fluffed around her cheeks, about as tame as gossamer, and the long robe swam on her slim frame. She was barefoot, holding Tommy's photo in her hand.

He saw the tears in her eyes. The emotion. The vulnerability.

"Hey," he said with alarm. But then remembered, of course, that she couldn't hear.

On the other side of the lamp was another photo. He grabbed it, showed her. In the picture, Tommy was a little older, but not so big that Maguire couldn't easily carry him around on his shoulders. Maybe they didn't look physically alike, and Maguire was certainly a lot older, but the photo should have showed her their relationship. He loved Tommy. He was as crazy about his half brother as Tommy had always been about him. They may have had different mothers, but they were unmistakably kin.

She saw. "So that's how you knew about me?" she asked. "Because of Tommy? Because you're part of Tommy's family?"

He nodded. Eventually that answer would undoubtedly raise more questions for her than it revealed… but it was still a punch of information that mattered. Her shoulders lost some of that stiff wariness.

It was a beginning.

Rather than grab the netbook and trying to type-talk to her, he figured he'd see how far they could get with sign language for a while. Would she like to go outside? Walk? He brought sweatpants and a sweatshirt for her to wear, boots she could pad up with thick wool socks, a jacket of his.

Initially she seemed to hesitate, but she shot such a longing look at the outside that he knew she was sold on the idea. It only took her a few minutes to take the makeshift clothes into the bathroom and emerge, looking like a homeless waif—but definitely a waif up for an adventure. The doctors had warned him that she needed serious rest and no exertion, but Maguire had to believe a little fresh air and sunshine would do her good.

Their first step outside, and he heard her chuckle, and saw how a natural smile transformed her face. Quail had hung out on the property for years, and this particular community of twenty-five or so looked exactly like what they were. Doofuses. Bobbing doo-fuses. They followed the leader, even when the leader was clumsy enough to trip on a rock and lead them through puddles.

A sassy wind blushed Carolina's cheeks, combed wildly through her hair. He grabbed her hand, climb-ing over a tall rock through the pines. Her eyes shot to his at the physical contact, but she didn't object.

A quarter-mile hike through pines led to a cliff

edge. It wasn't the best view, just a pretty vista—the mountains were getting a drench of snow in the distance, with a sunlit valley just below, salted with grazing deer.

Abruptly, though, he realized that he was still holding her hand, that they were standing hip-bumping close. His pulse gave an uneasy buck. The view was nice, but the way she looked at him, you'd have thought he'd given her gold.

He wanted—needed—Carolina to believe she could trust him, but those soft eyes conveyed something else. Something more. Something…worrisome.

Swiftly he dropped her hand. "Okay, Cee. That's enough exercise for today. The more fresh air for you, the better, but I think we'd better build up to it."

He forgot. She couldn't hear. But she seemed to respond to his intention, because she turned when he did, headed back down the trail. The last dozen yards, her face seemed to lose that wind-brushed color, and her eyes got that glazed, exhausted look again. He wanted to scoop an arm around her, but stopped himself just in time.

At the back door, he mouthed, "Nap for you," which provoked an immediate negative response. She shook her head frantically.

"No, Maguire. This is all too crazy. I need to know what's going on. Especially since I saw the picture of Tommy—"

Yeah, well. He was more than willing to talk with her, but first he had to get things back on the right footing. He got her inside, did the bossy domineering thing, yanking off her boots, settling her on the couch with a pillow and comforter, giving her a pad of paper so she could start working on those lists, then he got out of her way. His excuse for disappearing into the kitchen area was that he was making cocoa.

That turned out to be unnecessary. By the time he returned with a steaming mug of cocoa, brimming with melting marshmallows, she'd fallen asleep again.

He felt his stomach declench, his shoulder muscles loosen up. He'd made too much of that "look." Everything was fine. She needed to see him as a leader or a benevolent caretaker or someone who'd taken control of their situation. Actually, he didn't much care what label she gave him, or what she thought of him—as long as she didn't mistake him as a potential lover.

And obviously that wasn't a problem, if she could nap this easily. Everything was going hunky-dory, nothing to worry about, Maguire was sure.

Chapter Three

Maguire was quite a piece of work, Carolina mused. She needed to understand him, but figuring the man out was no easy task. Some of the puzzle pieces were definitely jagged fits. He was tough. He took charge and wanted everything his own way, and wasn't big on democracy in a household. He spelled "high-maintenance guy" in any language.

On the surface, he wasn't a man she'd normally like, much less be attracted to.

Carolina turned the page on her book. The office/library—no surprise—had whole shelves of books on birth defects related to brain function. Tommy had been one of those. And the room, like everything else in the lodge, was fabulous…three walls of fruit-wood bookshelves, a semicircular desk, little ladders to get to the top of the bookshelves, a couch and chair to sit in—and an old-fashioned fainting couch. The fainting couch was in a thick, suedey kind of fabric, and Carolina had taken one look and claimed it the minute she walked in here.

Nobody was getting her off that couch. Not Maguire. Not the army. No one or nothing. She was in love, and that was that.

In the meantime, dusk had already fallen. The day had passed amazingly fast—Maguire did some kind of work, but he'd left her upstairs with a pile of packages to sort through. Clothes. Not hers, but her size, nothing formal or fancy, just jeans and sweatshirts and socks, that kind of thing. And she'd napped. How on earth she could need more rest was beyond her, but apparently her body wanted to zone out every few hours, and there was nothing she could do about it.

Late afternoon, Maguire had pawed through the freezer, and come through with a gourmet French stew that just needed unthawing and heating to be savored. While he'd done that, she'd made her lists, but after dinner, she'd taken great pleasure in doing the dishes—primarily to give Maguire another fit. Apparently she wasn't supposed to do a thing for herself.

And after all that, they'd both settled in. She'd

pounced on her fainting couch with a book on special ed kids, while Maguire had taken the long couch, cocked his stocking feet on the trunk coffee table and was penciling through her lists. Initially he'd done so quietly, but Maguire being Maguire, eventually had to get a pen, a legal pad, to make notes and comments, and eventually he started muttering to himself. Probably because he still thought she couldn't hear.

"Lobster. Crab. Lobster. Scallops. Hmm. I'm sensing a common theme on your food list. Salmon from Alaska, only *really* from Alaska. Fresh sweet corn straight from a farmer's field. Blueberries right off a bush…for Pete's sake. Has no one ever fed you, girl…?"

He jotted some more scribbles on his legal pad. The last she'd peeked—less than a minute ago—no one had a prayer of reading his writing, including him.

"…Grape leaves. Stuffed, you know, the way the real Greeks do it. Actually, I don't know, tiger, but I get it that you want authentic. If you're going to be this easy to please, though, we're not going to have any fun. This isn't even challenging. And yeah, I know you can't hear me. But it's interesting, having a one-way conversation with a woman who can't talk back. Kind of every guy's favorite fantasy…well. Favorite fantasy separate from sex, of course…"

She could hear. Seeing Tommy's photo had jolted

something that morning…but not consistently. Her hearing, the volume of it, had gone in and out for hours now. It was only since dinner that she'd been able to hear anything consistently.

Once he'd hurled himself on the couch with her lists and started muttering, though, she'd heard every word.

She could have confessed that her hearing was back. She intended to come clean, eventually. Even little lies had always bugged her. But since she was distinctly at the most vulnerable disadvantage in this twosome, Carolina figured it was fair to find out what she could—any way she could. And there was an extraordinarily terrific side benefit to her deceit.

His voice.

Hearing the sound of his voice was like a powerful, free turn-on pill, with no risk and no side effects—beyond a tickle of her hormones. The pitch was low, not a bass, but definitely a low tenor, with a roll and timbre to his accent that put a shiver down her spine now and then. Sexy. He was just so altogether hopelessly, helplessly sexy. Those lethally blue eyes. Those all-guy bones of his, the overall look of him, the way he thought, the way he moved. It all came through in his voice. I am man, hear me roar.

It was that kind of voice. A baby-you're-gonna-love-how-I-kiss voice. A you-can't-imagine-how-much-trouble-I-can-get-you-into kind of voice.

It was mighty stupid, she knew, to travel even for a minute down that silly road. As sporadically as her hearing was returning, her memory seemed to be resurfacing the same way. Everything wasn't clear. But she'd recalled enough to make her want to curl up in a closet again, go back to where she'd become so agitated she couldn't keep food down, couldn't sleep, couldn't rest, couldn't escape. Anywhere.

So maybe it was irresponsible and downright dumb to dwell on Maguire's voice…but temporarily, it felt like self-preservation. Just listening to him allowed her to push her real life away for a little longer. It was hard to feel too guilty. Nothing was waiting for her in real life but more unsolvable problems and anxiety.

"Okay," Maguire mumbled. "Moving away from the food list and onto the major life wishes list. And right off the bat, cookie, I can see this list has more potential to be challenging…" He was still obviously talking to himself. He hadn't lifted his head from the legal pad. "You want to have dinner in a tree house. A real tree house. Hmm. You want fifteen pairs of Italian shoes. No surprise there—the shopping gene was bound to surface sooner or later. You want to sleep in a castle. A real castle. You'd like a weekend at a spa. Now you're talking. You want to ride in an old MG, like a '53, one of those 'darling ones' with running boards and all. You want…well, hey. Are you actually *listening* to this monologue, Carolina?"

Maguire had abruptly looked up. Looked straight at her.

He'd caught her. There was nothing she could do but fess up, so she nodded. "My hearing's coming back. I can't make it stay, but I've been listening to you talk. And I can hear my own voice. My hearing just seems to fade in and out. It's not consistent. I don't understand it."

"I do. The doctors all explained it the same way. You stopped hearing because your life had become an overwhelming pressure cooker. Remove the pressure, and there was every reason to believe you'd get your hearing back again."

"But nothing's changed." Anxiety nipped at her nerves, then took a serious raw bite. "The pressure and problems are all there, all real. In fact, I have to go home. I have to get up. I have to—"

When she made a move to push off the couch, he interrupted. His voice was quiet, calm. "I've got a deal for you."

"I'm not a make-a-deal kind of person, Maguire. There is no deal. As crazy as it sounds, I haven't minded being kidnapped, but now…it's all coming back. I don't have time to mess around. I have to go home—"

"Hold it, hold it. This is a deal that's going to work for you. I promise. You want to know how I happened to bring you here, don't you? So I'll fill in all the missing information. All you have to do is give me a chance to do that."

She hesitated. She did want to understand—fiercely—how this whole crazy thing had happened. But she wanted to hear about it right away, with no interruptions.

She should have known better. Everything had to be his way. He came through with a man's parka and hat and gloves for her, dragged her outside again. Early evening, the last color was just purpling the snow on the mountaintops. Not a breath of wind stirred. He helped her into an old Adirondack chair, buried in down blankets, but mittens out—so she could hold a glass of wine. Maguire started building a fire in a copper pit by the chairs.

It only took a few minutes before a blaze of golden sparks lit up the night. Wood smoke whiskered off in the valley, mingling with the pungent scent of pine. Maguire, wearing a leather jacket so old Goodwill would probably reject it, took the chair next to her, but his attention was on hunching over, stirring the fire, keeping it heaped up and hot.

And then he finally started talking. "Once upon a time," he said, "there was a man named Gerald who had three sons. Gerald's daddy had invented something so fantastic that he made millions, then billions, and Gerald inherited it all. He devoted his life to buying anything he wanted… That wine okay with you?"

"The wine's fine," she said impatiently. It was better than fine. It was some kind of fancy Pinot Noir, rich and dry and deep as the night. "Don't trying diverting me, Maguire. Keep talking."

"Okay, okay. Well, Gerald's first son was named Jay. Jay never worked, and probably never will. From the time he was sixteen, he was going through drugs and women, smashing fast cars, getting into every kind of trouble he could think of. He sounds rotten, but I swear you'd like him. Everyone does. He's a charmer."

Maguire checked her glass, saw she'd only had a sip or two, poured himself some, then went on. "Gerald went through that wife, then another. Eventually he had a second son. They got along like a snake and a mongoose. About the time Second Son was in college, he had a huge fight with his father because Gerald made a manslaughter charge against Jay disappear. Jay happened to be driving drunk, and hit an old man. The guy was homeless, so he didn't matter, right? No one knew him. No one missed him. The father couldn't figure out why his second son got his Jockeys in such a twist, but that was the last time Second Son spoke directly to his father."

Maguire paused for breath, but Carolina didn't comment. She'd stopped breathing altogether. For the first time in months, she easily put aside her own life and problems. It didn't take rocket science to figure out that Maguire was the second son, that he was talking about himself.

"A wife or two later, a third son came into the picture. Tommy was a complete surprise. Unfortunately, when Gerald's wife was eight months pregnant, he thought she'd enjoy taking a hang-glider ride. Apparently, they both did enjoy it, until the glider crashed. Gerald wasn't hurt, but his wife went into premature labor. She never made it out of the delivery room, lots of complications. Tommy lived, but he was born weeks too soon, was never right.

"Gerald solved the problem of Tommy like he did everything else. Threw money at it. The kid had full-time help at home, every toy ever made, was dragged to the best medical specialists on a regular basis. Since all the records pointed to the premature birth, the lack of oxygen—and maybe to the recreational drugs Gerald and his wife enjoyed—no one really expected to find miracles for Tommy. But at least there was no fear he wouldn't always be well taken care of."

Carolina watched him. He was restless now, couldn't sit still, had to fuss with the coals again, even though the fire was vibrantly shooting gold sparks into the night sky. "Last summer, Gerald put Tommy in a special place. He'd heard there was this really unusual summer program near South Bend, a school that had fresh ideas for the range of kids who just can't seem to progress because of their mental disabilities. Gerald wasn't really expecting Tommy to improve, of course. He just wanted to vacation in Corfu, wanted a place to stash him."

"Maguire." She said his voice softly, gently. She couldn't just let him go on, not when he was expressing so much hurt—in such a tough voice.

But he motioned her with a hand. "I know this is a long story, Carolina, but I really hate telling it. I'm almost at the end, so just let me get through it, okay?"

She nodded.

"So Tommy goes to this incredible place. And he has a seizure. Seizures aren't unusual for someone with Tommy's brain issues, but this teacher thinks there's something that doesn't make sense. So when an ambulance picks him up from the school, she goes to the hospital with him. Everybody starts getting mad at her. The doctor, the medical staff. They think she's interfering, full of herself, doesn't know anything. But the thing is, this teacher—by the name of Carolina Daniels—was right. All this time, there was actually a reason for a lot of Tommy's mental and physical disabilities. He had a tumor behind one eye.

"Now Tommy still isn't perfect. Never will be. But

his life just became damn close to normal, thanks to her. Gerald, being Gerald, offers her money. This Carolina woman won't take it. But that's all Gerald has ever known how to do—throw money at problems— so he puts her in his will, leaves this unsuspecting teacher somewhere around fifteen million dollars. Of course, Gerald wasn't actually planning on dying. But whatever. Gerald wanted her to have some payback, and being Gerald, he got what he wanted."

Maguire finally tried stretching out his long legs toward the fire, leaning back in the chair. "My guess is that our mysterious teacher—Carolina Daniels— was initially thrilled about the money. I mean, hey, who wouldn't be? Isn't that everybody's dream, to have total financial security, financial freedom, never have to worry about money again? Only, it didn't seem to work out quite that simple for her…" For the first time since he started talking, he shot her a glance. "You cold?"

"No, not at all."

"We're going inside the minute you're cold. You hungry?"

"No."

"More wine?"

"No. Good grief."

"Okay then. We're getting to the last part of the story. The awkward part. Here's the deal. The second son was always an interfering son of a gun. Self-righteous. Thinks he knows everything. That kind of pain-in-the-neck type of character. But he happens to really love his little brother. And even though Tommy's got a trust set up that will protect him forever financially, that second son has always been a part of Tommy's life. So that's how he knows about this teacher of Tommy's. How she saved Tommy's life. How she inherited that nest egg from Gerald."

Carolina opened her mouth, closed it. She had to let him finish.

"Okay. So Second Son—even though he hasn't got a legal right in the universe, even though it's none of his business in any way, even though he doesn't have time to mess around with a stranger's life—tracks down this Carolina Daniels. I don't know what you call that. Guilt? Lunacy? Trying to fix the sins of the father? Whatever. Second Son gets the impression that maybe this teacher isn't the toughest nut on the tree. In fact, this new, fabulous fortune isn't working at all like the fairy tale's supposed to be. Her money's brought out every vulture and piranha in the area. She's never had to cope with sharks before. She's never been trained to deal with greed at this level—or what levels people will fall to—to get a cut out of her. All that money, but she can't get safe. She can't…"

Carolina was still listening, but some of his monologue made her zone out. Her heart suddenly felt hugely full, brimming over. She still didn't have all the answers she wanted, and she hadn't had time to phrase even half the questions she wanted to. But he'd told her enough.

Her kidnapper was a good man. Better than a good man. Maguire was a true modern-day white knight who actually stepped up for damsels in distress— even if she wasn't a damsel, much less the kind of woman who counted on a man to save her from anything. Carolina never needed saving, anyway. She'd just desperately needed two seconds to think, to put her new life together, and there hadn't been a single stretch where she could hide from the bombardment of ceaseless pressures and demands being made of her.

"Maguire?"

"Yeah?" His voice edgy, wary now.

"You know I thought Maguire was your last name. You never once let on your real last name was Cochran."

He answered, "Well, hell. I didn't want you to have a negative impression right off the bat. It's not like I had any choice over the family I was born into. Believe me, I would have chosen Smith. Or Jones."

She got it, that he was hoping she'd laugh off the "little deceit" he'd pulled on her. But she couldn't stop thinking. "I kept trying to understand why I felt an... instinctive trust for you. Why I wasn't more afraid. I mean, for Pete's sake, you *were* kidnapping me."

"Borrowing," he corrected her swiftly. "Less prison time if we use a little different term than kidnapping."

"I had every reason to think you'd be after my money. Because everyone's been after my money. So why would you have taken me if not for ransom? It's the conclusion any sane person would come to, wouldn't you think? But it just didn't make sense in my mind. It just didn't...fit."

"You've been pretty drugged up, cookie. You shouldn't be expecting yourself to think rationally or normally for a while yet."

"Maybe. But I still knew. Somehow. That you weren't going to hurt me. That this wasn't about your wanting something from me." She leaned forward. "Maguire, how's Tommy?"

"Good. He's in Seattle. I petitioned the court for custody after my dad died, but as I mentioned, Gerald and I had issues. Dad did a good job of financially protecting him, but that's the best I can say. I see him at least twice a month, and sometimes he stays with me for weeks at a time..."

"So who is he with?"

"As odd as it sounds...with Jay's ex-wife. One of Jay's ex-wives. Shannon. The one thing Tommy needed that no amount of money could give him was a plain old mom. The nurturing of a mom, the warmth of a mom, the parenting relationship of a mom. He's crazy about Shannon. So it isn't a blood tie, but probably that's best. The Cochrans aren't exactly famous for their maternal or paternal judgment."

"So she volunteered for this? She's good with—"

From nowhere, in that quiet night, over the sparks of fire and zesty scent of pine, she suddenly heard a sound. A phone. A cell phone. Nothing more than that…but she instinctively responded as if she'd heard a rifle shot. She curled up, froze, covered her head.

"Carolina, it's okay, it's okay…I'll turn it off. Hell. I forgot I even had it on me…"

But there seemed to be an invisible mute button in her head that was punched hard. She stopped hearing the phone. His voice. The crackle of fire. It was gone again. Her whole sense of hearing.

She was back in that closet of silence, where no sound seemed to penetrate and nothing got through. She could feel herself shaking, a deep trembling from her fingertips to her lips. Her heart started pounding, pounding, as if she'd been running for her life and just had no breath left, nowhere to hide, nowhere to go.

She saw Maguire leaning over her, saw his mouth move. Was fairly positive his lips framed a mighty annoyed swearword. But that was all she could figure out for some time…

* * *

Within an hour of Henry's arrival, Maguire had the central dining table spread out with contracts, correspondence and various legal documents that supposedly required his immediate attention.

When Henry got in, he took one look at his boss's face and headed silently for the refrigerator. After inhaling every lunch food in sight, he'd poured a coffee, located himself against the counter and was being silent as a tomb. Possibly he'd worked for Maguire long enough to sense when his boss was crabbier than a bear with a sliver.

Maguire hadn't slept. He couldn't imagine sleeping in the near future.

This whole plan wasn't working. Well. Actually, it'd been working really well until Carolina heard the damn cell phone last night.

That she'd lost her hearing again wasn't the frazzler. Two different doctors had told him that could happen, and was even likely to happen. She had to be completely removed from stress for a serious stretch of time. The phone was a trigger for her.

She'd get her hearing back. That wasn't the problem. The problem was him. Instead of seeing her as a responsibility—a job, something he had to do—he kept feeling a pull toward those heart-big blue eyes. He touched her or tucked an arm around her, and just like that, he was harder than a teenage boy. That tangle of sizzle and rush happened every damn time they were in the same room.

He needed her to trust him. Which meant he had to earn that trust. And he sure as hell couldn't do that if she was afraid he was going to jump her.

Which, of course, he wasn't.

It was a matter of her never guessing that was even a remote possibility in his head.

"Where is she?" Henry risked asking a question, although he was still keeping a wary distance, still had his aviator jacket on.

"She's upstairs. I heard the shower a little while ago." He zoned in on the documents in front of him again—or tried to. The problem was that there were repercussions when he failed to concentrate on what mattered. If he failed to pay prompt attention to all this business, for example, he could lose a lot of money.

Unfortunately, he couldn't seem to give two shakes about losing money. He'd learned long ago that there were far worse things.

"Henry, you need to sleep over before flying again."

"Yes, sir."

"About all the issues we discussed regarding Carolina's place…"

"All done. Except that I also took the initiative of hiring a housesitter—actually, a concierge service—because I barely got to her place before there were people knocking and pounding and calling. She has some frantic relatives."

"I'll bet she does. Excellent judgment on getting the concierge service on board."

"Her sister, particularly, I believe, expected to be let in. Said Carolina had some things that were hers that she was supposed to get—"

"Right." Maguire didn't snort. He just thought about it. "If her family has any type of medical financial need, take care of it. Or call me. Otherwise nothing gets removed from her place except for old food in her refrigerator. Her bills and personal business—any crises there?"

"No. I canceled a dentist appointment for next week. And she has a hair appointment next Thursday."

"Hair." For the first time Maguire looked up, alarmed. "You know how women are about hair."

"Not exactly, sir."

"Nothing puts women in a bad mood faster than a bad-hair day. I don't even know what a bad-hair day is, exactly, but if that's a source of stress, we have to fix it."

"How, sir?" Henry asked.

"Damned if I know." Maguire dived into the

next stack of files. "Any men calling her?" he asked casually.

"Yes, sir, I told you—"

"I mean besides dentists and drugstores and insurance salesmen. The other kind of men. Boyfriends. Relationships."

"I don't think so." Abruptly Henry tugged on an ear. "Mr. Cochran, I don't recall you asking me to notice or collect information on anything regarding boyfriends. I wasn't looking for that. It never crossed my mind that you wanted me to."

"I didn't. And of course I didn't ask you. It's none of my business. It just occurred to me—a little late— that I should have considered whether or not she had a man in her life. You've seen her. Hard to believe there aren't man friends in that picture. And if it were *my* woman who disappeared from sight, I'd have raised hell and the National Guard and the Mormon Tabernacle Choir and the BBC—"

"I get your drift, sir. Possibly there just aren't any personal relationships in her life right now."

"Maybe." Maguire kept thumbing through documents. "In the meantime, I have a new list of things for you to do. Some of these are going to be fun."

"Fun," Henry repeated, and tugged on his ear again.

"Fun," Maguire repeated. "I need a l953 MG Mark IV TD here seven days from now."

"Seven days?"

"Red."

"Oh, that'll make it easier."

"Then I need you to locate a tree house. Not a kid's tree house. The kind of tree house where adults could live. I don't care where in the world. I just need one."

"That must be on your list of 'more fun' things for me to do, I suspect." Henry inked that in his Moleskine notepad, never blinked.

"Smile, Henry. Where else could you possibly work, where you had a job with this kind of diversity?"

"Nowhere, sir. There's no doubt in my mind."

"All right. Now...I'll be reachable most of next week, but primarily through my laptop. I can call you back, but I won't have a cell phone turned on, until I'm specifically looking for messages, so connection via the internet will be more predictable. I'll be in Europe for the next four or five days—I'm not sure of the exact stretch of time. It depends on what she's physically up for. To start off, I want to keep her away from disruptive noise as much as I can."

"But she can't hear, sir."

"Oh, yeah, she can. She hears too much. That's

the core of the problem, Henry. The point, however, is that I can't give you a complete schedule of where I'll be. I need to see how the next week goes with her. For her. Then some type of pattern should emerge."

"You don't need me for that week?"

"I need you all week. But for projects. I'll catch a ride on the Cochran business jet."

For the first time, Henry's face showed expression. "You know I can fly that—"

"Yes. I know you love flying anything. But I really need someone that I can completely trust on this—someone who can keep their mouth buttoned. You're one of the few in the universe. This is going to take some major finagling to pull off."

"Personally, I think it takes a man who's out of his mind, sir."

"Yeah, that, too. You know, I'm surprised the sister didn't threaten to sue—"

"She did, Mr. Cochran." Henry looked alarmed. "Didn't I already tell you that?

"You'd have gotten around to it. And there'll be more problems like that, for darn sure. Don't let it get your liver in an uproar."

"I don't drink, sir. My liver is almost never in an uproar. On the other hand—" Henry suddenly shot to an upright posture, looking in the doorway.

And there was Carolina, carrying a paperback, a

blanket draped over her shoulders, barefoot, looking like a waif.

A waif.

Not a femme fatale. Not a cocky confident woman who knew her way around men and valued her own allure.

A damn waif.

Yet his pulse started slamming as if an alarm just went off.

Chapter Four

Considering that her entire life had turned into a massive, uncontrollable disaster, Carolina couldn't believe how well she'd slept.

It was almost noon before she opened her eyes—and then she had to shake the clock, certain it had to be broken.

For the first time in weeks, though, she woke up charged—maybe not ready to climb mountains—but definitely in a hustle to yank on clothes and rush downstairs.

Halfway down the steps, she spotted Maguire sitting at the big table. One look, and her heart caught on a snag of emotion. Everything he'd told her last night had echoed in dreams, wild dreams, good dreams, all with the same underlying theme. She wasn't the only kidnappee. Maguire had had his soul kidnapped a long time ago, was stuck with an unpaid ransom just as she was. She had huge things she wanted to say to him today, huge things she wanted to do.

But abruptly she realized he wasn't alone. Another man was standing at the kitchen counter—Henry, she thought his name was. He was the man who'd piloted the jet, but also who just seemed a critical employee for Maguire, from everything she'd sensed and seen so far. When she called out a cheerful "Hello!" though, his cheeks flushed like a boy's.

Henry might be ultra-shy, but Maguire surged out of his chair as if jet-shot and jogged toward her. "Carolina! I was afraid you'd gone into a coma. You have to be starved. Or thirsty. Hell, I forgot, you lost your hearing again. Wait two shakes until I grab the netbook—"

She didn't sway because of dizziness or illness or anything like that. She was just stepping toward him, trying to make an instinctive calming gesture, when she seemed to trip over…nothing. Air. Her own feet. A speck of dust.

You'd have thought she'd started a fire. Maguire shouted something to Henry, grabbed her, swept her into his arms and started chugging with her up the stairs.

"Maguire—" Whether she could hear him or not, she was pretty sure there was nothing wrong with his hearing. Right then, though, he wasn't listening to her or anyone else. He was too busy having a fit and a half.

He charged with her into the bedroom, laid her on the bed as if she were breakable china, put a hand on her forehead while he was scooping covers over her at the same time. At the rate he was going, she was going to be smothered, either from excess heat or the weight of covers. It was pretty darn obvious he thought she was weak and sick and traumatized.

Hell's bells, maybe she was all three of those things, but the hysterical-deafness thing was getting beyond exasperating. At that precise moment, all Carolina wanted to do was communicate—that she was okay, that she wasn't in some new state of trauma, she'd just clumsily tripped over her own feet.

She didn't set out to kiss him. It was just…a kiss seemed a way to halt him in his tracks.

It worked beautifully.

Sort of.

All she did was frame his face in her hands, lift up and press her lips against his for a couple of seconds. That was all it took for Maguire to go from manic-energy machine to statue-still.

There was an unexpected repercussion. Her heart suffered immediate cardiac arrest. With that first contact, her lips seemed to instantly recognize that Maguire was nothing like any man she'd ever known. Her whole body knew it a millisecond later.

She'd felt so trapped these last two months, caged so tightly she couldn't seem to free herself. Maguire had inserted himself in the role of her white knight— alias her kidnapper—but that wasn't the man she found herself kissing.

It wasn't a hero who kissed her back.

It was a man who wasn't used to having his cage doors rattled. A man who didn't expect himself to… respond. A man who was used to initiating action, to controlling it, but not to ever, ever be on the receiving, unprepared end of it.

Carolina perceived all that on a swoop of sensation. Then other instincts completely took over.

The taste of him was dangerously exotic. Unfamiliar. Her heart bucked as if she'd been caught petting a tiger. She saw the flash in his eyes—a flash of alarm, awareness—just as she was closing hers. She'd never experienced it before. That spice of danger. She'd always been impulsive, enthused about taking the unknown road, exploring something different. With special children, she tried anything she could possibly think up, no matter how unconventional, to reach them. But that was about life in general.

It wasn't about men.

Yet when she felt the gruff whiskers on Maguire's

cheek and neck. Felt the pulse in his throat throb under her touch. Felt the satin-smooth texture of his mouth. Smelled him. His soap, the wood smoke he carried from their fire outside, nothing that yelled of a specific scent…except that he was male. Five-hundred-percent male.

.She didn't know any other five-hundred-percent males. Maybe there weren't any. Maybe this was the only male in her particular universe who pushed certain triggers that had never been pushed before, who aroused a cacophony of sensations that she hadn't realized existed before. She didn't think those things. She just sort of felt…awash. In him. His presence, his textures, his scent.

He broke free from the kiss connection, reared up his head, looked at her with a frown—a frown darker than a thundercloud. He started to speak, then seemed to remember she couldn't hear, and started to shake his head to communicate that way.

She went back for another kiss.

He'd been the kidnapper, but he didn't have all the power. She hadn't had any power in a long, long time. She'd been overwhelmed by everyone and everything. She was sick of it.

Being overwhelmed by sensation, now, was a different thing. That she could have power over him was enticing. Beyond enticing. She'd never remotely experienced feeling wicked before. She discovered that she liked it.

Possibly his back was breaking from the contorted posture he'd been trying to maintain, because when she surged up to try another kiss, to steal another taste, he suddenly lost all that perfect control of his. One second, she was sweetly claiming his mouth… the next second, he'd taken a dive into the bed, on her, with her. In a swirl and twist of covers, she was suddenly tangled with him, length to length, his arms swooped around her this time, his mouth taking hers.

One of her arms got trapped between the tussle of blankets and bodies. It wasn't fair; he had both his arms free, one slivering through her hair, then stroking down her back, kneading and rubbing, spine to hip and back up again.

He kissed differently than she had. His kisses involved tongues and teeth. Pressure. Invitation. Demand. The I-Want was bold, not subtle, out there like an open plane door, a chance of skydiving with no parachute, all risk, all…

All wonder.

All thrilling wonder.

"Hey." He broke away suddenly, breathing like a racing engine. "We can't…you can't…I can't—hey." His face was flushed, his eyes on fire. For her. At her. His face looked as fierce as a warrior's—but definitely not a happy warrior as he pushed up and away from her. He yanked the sheets up to her neck, and then hurled out of bed as if a fire were chasing him.

For a few seconds he stormed around the room, then whirled back, pointing the royal finger at her. The gesture for no was certainly crystal clear. Then he went out the door and slammed it.

Apparently this hearing thing was going to come and go indiscriminately, because she definitely heard the door slam. She could probably have heard it in Siberia.

Carolina wasn't sure what was going on—what she was doing, what she was risking or not risking. But she was positive about one thing. Her kidnapper was a fine man.

She'd heard his story, about how he'd been estranged from his father and family for a long time. Except for Tommy. And Maguire knew her story, at least the part about her helping Tommy, and the how and why his father had left her with such an extraordinary hefty inheritance.

So Maguire certainly wasn't a kidnapper in the usual sense. He had more money of his own than he could ever need. And he obviously didn't begrudge her the chunk from his dad, since he'd been treating her like a pampered princess.

She pushed up from the pillow, thinking that she'd

learned a lot of information….yet seemed to have even more questions than she had before.

She kept having the strangest feeling…that Maguire was the one who needed her, instead of the other way around. Of course, that didn't make sense. Her head still wasn't right. Her heart, her head, her whole body seemed to be nonstop exhausted, in some fuzzy state where she couldn't think clearly no matter what.

Like now. With her mouth still feeling bruised from his kisses, her skin feeling electrified where he'd touched, that sense of impending fall-off-a-cliff still skimming through her blood…she closed her eyes and inhaled an amazing sense of contentment. She felt hungry for the first time in weeks. Within her, a smile was starting from the inside out, for the first time since she could remember.

Clearly she was still weak and crazy, and Maguire was the voice of sanity.

But just for that instant…it didn't feel that way.

Two days later, Carolina found herself on a plane. Not the same fancy private jet they'd flown on before. This one was bigger, had a pilot and copilot up front, and a third man who'd been functioning as a butler, bringing platter after platter from the jet's galley.

Wilbur, the butler, had elegant white hair, the impeccable posture of a British lord, a face carved in strict expressionless lines and a fabulous wink. He'd started serving their dinner ten minutes ago. It was still coming. The table set up between her and Maguire was heaped with dishes. Lush bowls of hot butter. A tray of tools. Massive bowls of king crab. And initially, of course, bibs bigger than nightgowns.

Maguire was eating with her. But he wasn't talking. He'd barely said a word to her since those unexpectedly wild kisses two mornings ago. He'd been running around nonstop, scowling half the time, acting ultrabusy. He'd used the netbook to inform her they were flying east, a good trip, not to worry.

She wasn't worried and hadn't asked. She'd wanted to think about that unexpected sexual encounter herself before tackling Maguire again. But once they started stuffing themselves with the rich, juicy, succulent crab—one of her favorite meals in the universe—she started talking.

"My hearing's coming back again," she announced.

He looked up. "Good."

He added nothing else, but that was fine with Carolina. She wanted to be the one to direct the conversation this time.

"I was hoping you wouldn't mind telling me some more about how Tommy's doing."

He hesitated, but not for long. "Since last summer,

I think you'd find his progress has been amazing. He'll never be normal—"

"Normal's a meaningless word, as far as I'm concerned. He was always happy by nature."

"He still is. But he's talking now. Not perfectly, but he's able to communicate. He stopped having the seizures, the fierce headaches. Something is seriously weird about his brain wiring. Nobody seems to be able to completely identify or fix it. But he's amazingly better, thanks to you, with a much happier picture for a future."

"I wasn't looking for thanks, Maguire. I just remember him. I care what's been happening with him."

Maguire was far more skilled at handling the crab than she was.

She had to work twice as hard to scoop out half as much of the sweet white meat—but damn. It was fun.

"My father always claimed to love Tommy, but his method of caring was to throw treatments and programs at him. Nothing was too expensive. But typical of my dad, that meant that Tommy was primarily seen and raised by various professional people. Strangers. Not people who were really listening to him, looking at him, day by day. You listened."

"Quit it, Maguire. I wasn't looking for praise or thanks. I wanted to hear more about the progress he's made since the surgery. What programs he's part of now."

He nodded. "Hopefully, sometime over the next couple weeks you'll get a chance to see him."

"Really? I'd love that." For a few seconds she was diverted from eating the butter-dripping crab. "I'm not sure if he'll still remember me, but—"

"Trust me. He remembers you."

Wilbur had brought bowls, warm water with squeezed lemons, for them to wash their hands. She didn't want to give up eating, but she didn't expect to have Maguire trapped like this forever. So she rinsed, wiped, removed the gigantic bib and sat back. "You're clearly happy with what I did for Tommy. But I still find it upsetting that you leaped into my life since I turned into…well, into a fruitcake. So I'd like to explain the fruitcake thing."

"You don't have to."

She said quietly, "Yeah. I really do." She took a breath and then just started in. "The day the lawyer called, to tell me about the inheritance, I was… beyond stunned. Obviously I know I helped your little brother. But it's not as if I did anything brave or spectacular. It was just…luck. I work with enough special kids to notice those different symptoms in Tommy."

"Luck might have been part of it. But you cared

enough to step in. To fight for him," Maguire said brusquely.

"Well. Whatever. The point is…everyone in my world was thrilled for me. My parents. My sister. Aunts and uncles, friends, everyone. We never had much growing up, so the first thing I did for my dad was buy him a new car. He'd never had a new one before. He always bought used, so new was a treat. And my mom…for years she'd been dreaming about having a new kitchen with a double oven. I started out having so much fun with the money, I can't begin to tell you. Only, that changed. Pretty quickly."

Maguire finally finished eating, sank back while Wilbur took away the evidence of their feast and then disappeared into the front cabin with the crew. Carolina doggedly talked on.

"I started getting nonstop calls. One was a school for special kids, who wanted me to donate the money for a wing. Then my dad. He got really upset because he thought I should make him into my manager, instead of hiring an accountant. Then my sister…she asked me to fund her two kids' college educations. I did. In fact, I was happy to do that. Only…it just went on and on…"

Maguire handed her a soda, as if sensing her throat was dry.

It was. But that didn't stop her from talking.

"I had one second cousin—twice removed—who

had a son who got in trouble with the law. I'm not trying to be funny. The relationship was so distant that I barely knew who he was, and I had only met him once in my life. But he wanted me to pay the attorney fees. Then my sister wanted a new house. I was getting phone calls almost 24/7. Life insurance. Security. Real-estate people. Stockbrokers. Cancer, heart, diabetes, prosthetics, Lou Gehrig's disease... I'm not sure how all these strangers knew I'd gotten this inheritance. And they're all good causes, Maguire. Things I do care about. But my life just got...insane. I couldn't take a bath or read a book. I couldn't come home at all, without the phone ringing or someone pounding at the door." She lifted a hand. "I woke up one morning to find a homeless woman on my doorstep."

Maguire didn't interrupt, just kept looking at her with those silvery blue eyes, as if the only thing on his mind or in his heart was to listen to her.

"For a while, I was still teaching. I mean, I thought my life would basically be the same. Sure, I'd have this fabulous nest egg and some luxuries, but I was still a teacher at heart. It's who I am, what I do. Only, the kids I teach are uniquely vulnerable, so when strangers started bugging me at school, the kids were affected. The principal gave me a five-star review for my job performance, yet at the same time he suggested I leave. Everything was different. People, my friends, the other teachers… I was expected to pay if we went out to lunch. Or I wasn't included because I was suddenly perceived as different. I had men calling me. Men I'd never met. Men I never wanted to meet. And then there was a break-in—it was just weeks after the inheritance. I hadn't really made many changes in my apartment. Well, some. The one thing I did pretty quickly was get a new computer, because mine was six years old and I was getting the blue screen of death all the time—"

Maguire shot her a look. He didn't roll his eyes, but she got the gist.

"Okay," she said, "I know I'm digressing. The break-in was the point. It really shook my timbers. But even worse was the steady round of lawyers and security people calling after that. And I forgot. There was a neighbor who came over, lost her husband, was hoping I could pay her rent for a while. Then… my father's second aunt's grandson's wife was pregnant with a baby that needed some kind of expensive operation—"

"Carolina?"

"What?"

"I know all this," he said patiently. "I'm surprised you didn't cave long before you did. The way the doctors explained that 'hysterical deafness'…it was your body giving you permission to shut down and quit listening to everyone's demands. Losing your hearing was self-defense."

"Whatever. Here's the thing I wanted to say. You know what? This is really your family's money. Not mine. Why don't I just give it back to you."

"No. Not an option."

"Just listen to me, all right? I've lost just about everything that matters to me. My job. The family relationships I thought were strong and solid. Friends. The things I loved to do, loved to be part of, always took for granted. And you know what?"

Maguire wiped a hand over his face, tucked his chin on a fist. "What?"

"When you first kidnapped me, I kept thinking how weird it was...that I wasn't afraid. But now I actually get it. Because my reality is that I couldn't bé a happier kidnappee. I don't want to go home right now. I really don't."

"And you're not."

"But all those problems'll go away if you just take the money back. Wouldn't you like all those millions?" she asked coaxingly.

Maguire got this expression on his face as if he were fighting not to laugh. Fighting to believe she was for real. "I have more than enough money than I could ever use or want, Cee. So, no."

"Okay then. How about for Tommy? How about if I give it all to Tommy?"

"Tommy couldn't use another penny in his lifetime. He's got a fortune. All in safe, secure trust funds."

Still. She was warming up to the idea. "You could burn it if you wanted to. Or throw it away. I always thought I wanted heaps of it. That it'd be so much fun to buy anything I wanted. That I'd feel so much safer if I had security in the bank. And that's been the craziest part. It's not fun. And I don't think I'll ever feel safe again."

"Yes, you will," he said quietly, forcefully. "You can make different choices—"

"I know, I know. I could always choose to just give it all away. And in principle, I'd love to do that. To pick people and causes who really needed something, or someone, to come through for them. Only, Maguire, I learned the hard way that it'll never be like that. Because no matter who I give to, someone else will be mad that it wasn't them. Or mad that I didn't give enough."

"But there's still another choice—"

"I know, I know. You think I haven't thought this through? I could start all over under an assumed name. That has a lot of appeal. You probably think it's the best choice. I mean, I've been whining about what awful people my family and friends have turned into, haven't I? But I just can't see giving them totally up quite yet. I mean, they're my whole history. Warts and all, they're still my blood. Maybe my life is broken right now…but getting even more broken doesn't make any more sense, does it?"

"No. And there really is another choice, Carolina."

"What?"

But just then Wilbur emerged from the front cabin, ordering them to strap in because they were "imminently landing."

For the first time in hours, she glanced out the window. She hadn't asked where they were going—didn't really care—and her internal time clock was so topsy-turvy that she didn't have a clue what time it was. But there was some kind of ambient pale light outside, enough to reveal breathtaking, snow-covered mountains, higher than any she'd either seen or dreamed of.

"Where *are* we?"

"In the air," Maguire said dryly.

She flashed him a look. "I might just sock you on general principle. Answer the question."

"We're at one of the places that's going to help you find the answers you're looking for."

"I hate cryptic. Just so you know."

"All right. I'll answer you straight. We're going to a place where you're going to get good and muddy. Muddier than you've ever been in your entire life."

"Muddy? Huh?"

Chapter Five

He meant it. The crazy man actually meant it. Carolina remembered the lists he'd made her create, that somewhere she'd mentioned wanting to sleep in a real castle, something else about wanting a spa weekend. At the time, she'd thought the whole thing was a joke. Nothing anyone would take seriously.

Yet the green mud completely slathering her body was unquestionably real.

And so was the castle.

"You're not too cold, mam'selle? Too warm?"

"I'm perfect," Carolina assured the tall Amazon with the serene blue eyes and hands of steel.

"Are you thirsty? Would you care for a drink?"

The last time she'd admitted to thirst, Greta had given her some god-awful herbal concoction that made her eyes sting and her tongue pucker. It wasn't safe around here to admit wanting or needing anything.

"I'm fine," she said.

"All right. Now, you close your eyes. I'll be back in thirty minutes, after the clay has set."

The mud-clay had already started setting. She was increasingly feeling like a naked mummy. A naked green mummy. The castle was located in the Alps—whether Swiss or French or Italian, she had no idea. But it was perched on a cliff top, accessible only via helicopter, and the once-classic structure had been turned into an elegantly exotic spa. The place had a great room draped with impossibly tall silk tapestries. The fireplaces in half the rooms were bigger than she was. The floors were all stone or marble, but heated beneath the floor, so it was warm walking around, even in bare feet. Fountains decorated almost all the rooms, as did candles. The view outside was of treacherously tall mountains, draped with a white ermine cape of snow. Inside was luxury, pampering, softness, gentle music.

"You're surviving in there, Cee?"

She heard him. Maguire's sexy tenor was unmistakable. He was in the next room—sort of an anteroom he'd turned into a makeshift office. It had a laptop, printer, fax, all the usual office suspects, although she hadn't once heard a telephone ring. She concluded Maguire had forbidden telephones anywhere near her.

He'd disappeared from physical sight, once the Amazonian Greta had shown up to slather her in mud and seaweed. He was just within calling distance, and asked how she was doing on a regular basis.

He hadn't looked. Not the whole time she'd been stripped down, gooped up, smoothed, encased in oils and warm towels and then this clay-mud thing. It was more than a little weird, being naked with strangers. But enticingly weird, knowing Maguire was in the next room, always close enough to call for him.

It was impossible not to be aware that she was naked. That he knew it.

Of course, she was coated in green slime, so heaven knew why sex was on her mind. Probably he'd run for the hills if he saw her.

"Doing good. You getting business done in there?"

"Yeah. Funny world today. It doesn't really matter where you are, it's not that hard to communicate with anyone at any time from any place."

"Maguire."

"Yeah?"

"You set this up because it was on my list."

"Well, yeah. It was an easy twofer. You wanted to sleep in a castle. And do the spa thing."

"I want my list back."

"Nope."

"I thought it was a game. Just something silly. I don't want or expect anything else from that list."

"Uh-huh. Damn, I seem to have a fax coming in, and need to do some business here for a while…"

Right. She believed the moon was made of cheese, too. Maguire somehow never answered questions he didn't want to answer. And even though she'd spent long days with him now, she still didn't know where he lived, or what he did with his time.

If he had a woman in his life.

Or what he'd thought of those kisses they'd shared a few days ago. She really wanted to know if they'd haunted him the way they were haunting her.

Temporarily, there was no possible way to address the idea. Greta showed up again, did more terrifying things. It took ages to rinse off all the mud, and then she was coated with warm spicy oils and rubbed down. After that, her feet and hands were encased in warm packs, and her hair coated with something that looked like mayonnaise and smelled like vanilla.

By the time she was starting to feel like a recipe, Greta let her shower the whole thing off. Her hair was dried, her toes and nails pampered. She was snuggled into a black, whisper-satin gown like the kind movie stars wore in the forties, warned that she'd need a good long nap after all the treatments, and put in a wrought-iron elevator.

Their suite was on the third floor. Carolina had no idea how many others were enjoying the spa, but so far she'd only seen staff—and Maguire. The suite took her breath the first time she saw it.

His-and-her bedrooms both had their own bathrooms. The central living area between held a fireplace, a medieval round table and a wall tapestry that concealed a minifridge with snacks and drinks. Her bed was on a pedestal, with velvet drapes and handembroidered pillows. Greta had told her the truth. She barely made it inside before folding up on the bed and sleeping hard and deep.

When she wakened, though, the sensation of luxurious pampering and contentment was gone. Her head was thudding, her heart pounding. The long, whispersatin gown still felt embarrassingly sexy against her skin, the heap of Swiss feather bed no less fabulous, but she headed into the main room, knelt down on the stone hearth.

This whole week had been disturbing and tantalizing and scary and wonderful, and above all, distracting.

But she had a life in shambles back home. It hadn't disappeared. Maybe she'd desperately needed a break. Maybe she could be excused for hiding out for a few days. But she'd done that now, and the crushing weight of decisions and problems was still waiting for her.

She had to push the stop button. She couldn't keep falling for a man who wasn't for her, living a fantasy life that wasn't hers…behaving like a woman she couldn't be.

Maguire disconnected from all electronics, locked down his business and headed upstairs. The staff claimed Carolina would likely take a solid two-hour nap, but he hadn't checked on her in a while now. He didn't want to make further plans for the day until he evaluated what she felt up to.

As the elevator let him out on the third floor, he considered that he wouldn't mind a serious nap himself. His neck creaked, and a sharp headache threatened around his eyes. He was used to lack of sleep, but he'd been pouring on work hours on top of time changes and travel.

Adding Carolina to his life had created all kinds of complications. Some, he'd expected. Some were mightily confounding him.

The door to their suite was an oval-shaped piece of carved wood—very cool and castle-like—but it was darned hard to unlock the door without making a sound. Still, he tried, let himself in, and then immediately stopped dead.

"Hey," he said, but he thought, Hell. Hell times ten.

Carolina wasn't sleeping the way she was supposed to be, but sitting on the hearth rug, her head on her knees, kind of rocking back and forth. Her toes peeked out of a gown that couldn't be legal in public. God knew every inch of her was covered—except for pale pink toenails. But the slinky-slidey material revealed every hint of curve. Her nipples. Her adorableness.

And he'd have been happy to concentrate on that, but it was downright impossible to miss her disconsolate posture. She had that look in her eyes again. The lost-waif look. The why-would-you-kick-my-puppy look.

"Hey," he said again, trying for his most blustery voice. Wary of making anything worse, he moved closer, crouched down next to her. "This isn't how the story's supposed to go. You were supposed to love all this. Sleeping in the cool old castle. All the history crud. The spa thing."

"I did. I do. But, Maguire, I just can't keep playing. I have to go home!"

Here he'd expected Armageddon from those anxiety-drenched eyes. Instead, this was nothing more than a little crisis. "Of course you're going home," he said, and leaned forward, to poke a long fork into the flames, push at the logs, creating a fireworks of sparks shooting up the giant chimney—and a spray of light that glowed on her skin. "Just not quite this minute. See, back home, you have all those people who want to bite off a piece of you. That's what happens when you inherit serious money. It brings out the vultures in people, even normally good people. And you know the real problem with that?"

"Everything."

"No." He hooked an arm around her shoulder—not too close—no fingers touching what they shouldn't. Just a hug-hook. Nothing more. "The real problem is that *you* got lost in that picture. All you've been hearing is what everyone else wants, what everyone else expects. We've got to switch that back, and make it about you. The money's a chance for you to say... what do you want from your life? What really matters to you? So we work on that stuff. We don't go back home until you know exactly what you want to do from here. You go back strong. You go back feeling good about yourself, your life, what you want. And until then, you get to hide out, and let Maguire— that's me—take care of all the crappy details."

"You're a goofy man, Maguire."

"I've been insulted worse. Trust me." He looked around, too damn aware of her warm skin, the scents surrounding her, that tousled brush of silvery-blond hair.

"I don't want to be...beholden to you. You don't

owe me anything, much less all the time you've been taking—"

"This isn't about owing. It's about understanding. I know exactly what that inheritance did to your life because I know exactly what it did to my own family. It's been sabotaging everything you could do or be. But I can stop that from happening to you. I can help you make it work."

"No, you can't."

"Actually, I can, Carolina. I can teach you to be tough. I can show you how to handle this, the way no one else can, because you know positively that I don't need or want anything from you."

She frowned. "You always sound so logical when you start talking. Only, what I'm saying is logical, too. No matter what I do, people are going to be unhappy with me."

"And that's a big deal, huh?"

"Maybe it wouldn't be for you. And I'm not trying to win a popularity contest like a thirteen-year-old kid, Maguire. I'm just trying to live a decent life. Do the things that matter to me."

Somewhere around here, there had to be some liquid refreshment that didn't involve sour-tasting herbs or mystery gray stuff that was "good for you." He got up, prowled around the various cupboards and shelves, found a carafe, sterling goblets, plain old bottled water. "I want you to think for a minute," he said.

"I am thinking." She also took the goblet of simple cool water and gulped it down.

"Back when you became a special ed teacher, you were influenced by what you believed you could do. That affected where you could go to college, the goals you had then, the places you applied for work. Essentially you established boundaries that worked for your life then—but now, you can take all that fencing away. Imagine, if you could have gone to any university on the planet, would you still have chosen the school you went to?"

She sipped more water. "That's impossible to know."

"Nope. That's the point. What was impossible before could be totally possible for you now. If you wanted—and still want—to do things for kids with special needs, you have a whole basketful of options to pick from these days. You can still teach, if that's what you want. But you could also start your own school for kids with special needs, if you wanted that. Or you could get a group of experts together, come up with entirely new program ideas for special-needs kids. There's no limit to where you could take just this one part of your life."

She frowned. "You're messing with my head, Maguire."

"And that's exactly what I want to do for a couple weeks. Mess with your head. Show you how to use that money instead of it using you. Help you get what you want."

"Maguire? What if I want something that you don't agree with."

"That's easy. This isn't about me. I don't have to agree with anything. If you want it, then we'll find a way to help you go for it." He thought the whole talk was going pretty well. Very well, in fact, but there was something in her expression that changed. She faced him, her soft eyes glued on his, studying, examining. Thinking. Thinking too much. It was obvious she was the kind of woman who got in trouble if she spent too much time thinking. "What?" he said impatiently.

"I could want to go after something, no holds barred, risk everything, that you'd really have a problem with."

"Like what?"

"Like what if I wanted *you,* Maguire? What if all I wanted was to fall in love with you?"

Her voice was softer than melted butter. He almost had a heart attack, but thank God, the phone vibrated in his pocket. He grabbed for it with a palm that was wet with sudden sweat—shock sweat—and could barely manage a coherent conversation.

The call only lasted a minute. By that time, he'd

managed to shoot to the other side of the room, with a massive old medieval table between them, which had to weigh five hundred pounds. Not that he was afraid of her. The waif? How could he possibly be afraid of the waif? He just felt more…secure…with a little distance between them. At least until he recovered from the words she'd blurted out. Especially that one word. The four-letter one.

"We can talk seriously. And nonseriously. About a lot of things." That was a promise. "But right now, there are some people coming up here."

"Wait a minute. What people? Why?"

Thank God they got here. Initially he'd been wary of setting up the Shoe Project, wary that Carolina wasn't ready for any commotion yet. But "Italian shoes" had been high on her wish list, and rather than spend time actually shopping in Rome or Milan—not his favorite pastime, for sure—he figured it'd be more time efficient to bring the products to her. It wasn't as if her shoe size had been hard to find out ahead of time.

He sprang up when he heard the first knock on the door, and then the parade began. Almost all the vendors were men, carrying boxes and carts, with labels like JP Tod, Miu Miu, Fendi, Versace, Casadei.

Carolina—the precariously fragile woman he'd found curled in a hospital bed in a fetal position—started shrieking like a child on a playground.

The scene deteriorated from awful to worse. Maguire hiked to the bar, grabbed a malt liquor and hastily retreated to a corner, out of harm's way. It only took minutes for their serene living space to turn into Armageddon. Boxes were opened, splayed. Carolina was fitted, argued over, and encouraged to walk up and down the room in various shoes.

He had no idea that shoes had their own language, but he kept hearing terms he'd never heard before, like "Dorsay pumps" and "kidskin with a Swarovski buckle" and "burgundy strapper." One Miu Miu was defined as a "feather shoe," which is exactly what it looked like—a bunch of silly feathers—so Maguire was confounded how the pair could cost five thousand bucks. A lavender sandal from Versace almost made Carolina drool—she was groaning like a woman in the throes of orgasm—and then came something identified as a red patent-leather lace-up. One look at that pair and she started giggling. And dancing around the room with the swagger of a goofy drunk.

En route, he accidentally noticed that he'd vastly underestimated her legs before. Maybe she was generally built on the scrappy side, but her ankles and calves and thighs….there was nothing wrong with those legs. They were toned, shaped perfectly, an erotic dream for a guy who had a leg fetish.

When his thoughts strayed in that direction, Maguire pulled those reins tight. This wasn't about him.

In fact, Carolina acting like a giddy, happy schoolgirl highlighted exactly what the real issues were about. She had a serious character flaw. That flaw was that she was a serious, hard-core, possibly unfixable softie. As far as he could tell, she was forever giving, always thinking of others, always looking to help others.

The world was going to kill her—particularly now that she had money—unless Maguire found ways to toughen her up. Her guileless warning that she could fall in love with him only echoed his own conscience. She had no defenses, not against feelings of the heart.

Only a manipulative user of a man would take advantage of that. He had to keep his hands off her.

Which was, temporarily, relatively easy.

"Maguire!" she shrieked. "What do you think?"

She paraded closer, lifting her robe to knee length so he had a better view of her right foot—in a purple crocodile heel—and her left foot, in a shiny red sandal thing.

"I think you're gonna kill yourself," he said gruffly. Both heels were four inches high or more. No one could walk in those things and live.

"Don't you think they're beautiful?"

"Oh, yeah." Maybe he hadn't seen it in the beginning, but now it was so obvious. When she smiled, she had an aura that lit up a whole room, a radiance that glowed from the inside out. He kept getting glimpses of how Carolina had been before the crippling inheritance—a happy-on-the-inside woman, a giggler, a joyful, uninhibited fun lover. He'd bet the bank she sang at the top of her lungs when she was alone in a car.

She teetered back to the shoe gurus, and tried on another pair...when something abruptly went wrong. He couldn't hear what was said over the commotion, but she abruptly put down a shoe and her face went blank. He crossed the room at a breakneck pace, asked casually, "Did some kind of problem come up?"

Her eyes shot to his. "That pair of suede pumps..." She motioned.

"The purple ones?"

"Yeah. Maguire." She put a hand on her heart. "I asked how much they were—$843! Holy kamoly. Holy moly. Holy smokes. Holy—"

He got it. Apparently she'd originally thought of Italian shoes as a luxury, but she never expected them to be this much of a luxury. "You can afford it," he said.

"That's not the point. I—"

He swiftly hooked an arm around her, so they could at least have the privacy of a conversation away from the hot-eyed vendors. Good grief, she was trembling. Flushed.

"One pair would pay for two months of groceries.

That's ridiculous, Maguire. It's a stupid use of money. Especially for something this...selfish. Something I don't remotely need. Look, when I put Italian shoes on the list, it was because I tried on these flats that a friend had—they were Italian, and they fit like a soft glove, and I never forgot how wonderful they felt. But that's all it was. A fantasy. And I'd never actually priced them before, because—"

Easy enough to guess the end of that line. "Because it never occurred to you to spend money on yourself."

"Well, of course I spend money on myself. But a ten-buck pair of earrings on sale at Kohl's is just a whole different world than this—"

He could feel the warmth of her skin, under his arm, the surge of protective instincts of a man for his mate, the instant strike of an erection just from being this close. Damn it. He said firmly, "Carolina. Buy one pair."

"I can't."

"Yes, you can. I dare you. Prove to yourself that the world will not end if you have a frivolous moment—"

"But—"

"I'll buy you *two* pairs—if you don't stand up for what you want yourself. That's wasting double the money."

Her jaw dropped in alarm. "Don't do that, Maguire! Don't buy me anything. There's no reason—"

He gestured back to the numerous shoe boxes. "Well, then pick a pair yourself. Or two. You can do it. I promise, it won't kill you."

"But, Maguire—"

"Go. Be strong. Be tough. Be mean."

"But Maguire—"

"The cost of two pairs of shoes is not going to solve world hunger. You're going to have lots of chances to do serious things with your money. But that has to start with you, giving yourself permission to make choices. That includes permission to smile, to have some fun. Permission to make choices that have nothing to do with anyone else's opinion."

Her shoulders sagged. "I hate it when you handle me. You're exhausting, Maguire."

Yeah, yeah. Getting that woman to do something selfish was like getting a nun to try mud wrestling. It took bullying and cheerleading and taunting and threats.

And after that, the whole situation only got worse.

Chapter Six

Sipping on a pineapple-mango cocktail—minus the alcohol—Carolina looked out the jet window and reflected that she'd learned tons about Maguire in the last twenty-four hours. She already knew his flaws. He could be dictatorial, manipulative, pushy. When the man got an idea in his head, nothing could make the blockhead back down.

But his absolute, unrelenting kindness was the stunner.

My God, she was falling in love with him. But it wasn't her fault. If it hadn't been for that pain-in-the-keester inheritance, she'd never have met him. He was so one of a kind. She'd never known anyone who worked so hard to hide positive character traits like kindness and compassion and caring. He put on such a strong front. How could she possibly have initially known that he was a man so worth loving? So full of love?

So alone.

"Hey, trouble."

Maguire, for a blissful twenty minutes, had been napping next to her in the aisle seat. She glanced away from the window, back at him. "Could you conceivably be speaking to me?"

His grin was as crooked as a thief's. "Uh-huh. I just wanted to ask—do you ever plan to take those shoes off?"

"Don't be silly, Maguire. A girl doesn't buy shoes like this and hide them away."

"Did you actually sleep in them last night?"

She heard the teasing. He thought the shoe thing was hysterically funny. Naturally she had to encourage him. "Let me put it this way. Where I go, the shoes go. If I'm not wearing them, then they're on their own pillow."

He took a sip of her drink and grimaced when he discovered it was without alcohol. "I just brought up the subject of the shoes again—"

"Because you can't let it go?"

"No. Not that. Because I thought you might want

to consider that just possibly they don't necessarily go with every type of attire."

"Of course they do." She glanced out the window again, distracted when the jet dipped low and started circling. Below was Monaco. It looked far more like a fairy tale than anything real. The city of Monte Carlo was wedged between aqua sea and mountains, with big white yachts framing the curve of the Côte d'Azur. The late-afternoon sun had drenched the background mountains in wet gold. Castle tops came into view, with their turrets and turquoise roofs, and endless splashes of flowering gardens and fountains.

When she turned back to Maguire, Carolina realized yet again that she must have lost her mind... because she'd rather look at him, concentrate on him, than that fabulous scene below.

"You didn't tell me how long we were going to be here."

"Because I'm not sure. The plan is only for a couple days, but we could stay a little longer, if you want. Tonight I had in mind dinner at the Ship and Castle restaurant, one of those landmark places right on the Côte d'Azur. The food's a little on the exotic side, but honestly, it's one of the best places on the planet. After that, I figured we'd make a run on the Monte Carlo Casino, where we'll see what a gambler you are." He sighed. "You don't have to drip diamonds at either place, but I'd say you'd feel the most comfortable in, like, a black dress kind of thing."

"Believe it or not, Maguire, I could probably have guessed that without coaching." She had to grin as he wiped a hand over his face.

"I was trying to help, I swear. I just wasn't sure if you'd want to wear those shoes with a formal black dress."

"They're not leaving my feet, Maguire. Get used to it." Her voice was firm, but her eyes softened when she looked at her feet. The red patent-leather lace-ups were Versace, cost in the ballpark of four hundred dollars. They weren't, even remotely, the most expensive shoes she'd looked at, but the cost still put them way, way up there in the Disgrace level. Still, they were the cutest thing she'd ever owned.

"Now," she began, thinking that now Maguire was finally awake, she had things to discuss with him. Her brain hiccuped when she caught Maguire staring at her shoes, too. Or possibly not at her shoes. His gaze seemed downright riveted on her calves and ankles.

"Now," she began again, but Maguire's fascination with her legs sent a ball of fire straight to her belly, distracting her. "I was wondering," she started for a third time, "whether the woman in your life isn't having a problem with your spending so much time with me."

Maguire didn't even blink. "Well, yeah, of course

she has a problem. But she's so well trained and obedient that she wouldn't think of expressing it." He kindly reached over to thwack her back when she started choking.

Thankfully she recovered quickly, even magnanimously resisted the urge to elbow him in the ribs. "So," she said, "there are no serious women in your life right now, huh. How could that possibly be?"

"Maybe...most women have better judgment in men than you do?"

"Can't be that. I have superior judgment in people," she informed him.

"Right. Pit you and a lamb against a lion, and the lamb'd probably be tougher. Way tougher."

"Good insult," she praised him. "But you're digressing. Were you ever married?"

"Did I realize that you were nosy before this?"

"Really? Not even married once?"

He glowered at her. "You were way, way easier to handle when you were deaf."

She was on to him. If she let him get away with his nonsense, it was the same as enabling the devil. So she stayed dogged on the subject. "I'll bet quite a few women gave you a run for their money."

"For my money, maybe. I've never gone after a woman for hers."

"Aha. You let some information slip out there,

Maguire. You're losing your edge." She winked at him. "Want to look at my gorgeous legs again?"

"Hey, did your parents never spank you? No one ever said, honey, don't touch a hot stove? Don't open the cage door of a bear?"

"Did yours? Is that how you got so wary? You're just too adorable to be alone, Maguire. There should be women snapping at your heels, doing inventive things to capture your interest, thrilled to make sure you never have to sleep alone at night."

He squinted at her in the sunlight, just as the pilot announced their imminent descent into Monaco. "You're getting way, way stronger faster than I thought you would, Cee. I'm beginning to think the shoes are a factor."

"Me, too. Think what red shoes did for Dorothy in *The Wizard of Oz*. Of course, all she wanted was to go home to Kansas."

Maguire said quietly, "And that's all you want, too, isn't it? Your reference point isn't Kansas. But you want the same thing Dorothy did. To find your way back home."

She thought about that on their drive to the hotel. Maguire was right. This crazy journey he'd taken her on was all about becoming strong enough to go home.

And the truth was…she felt stronger every day. Maybe she still had no clear plan about how to face all the dragons waiting for her at home, but she was starting to feel. Starting to stand up. Starting to own her heart again.

But she wasn't ready to leave Maguire.

Even if a broken heart was at the end of this journey, she'd come far enough—become strong enough—to be absolutely certain how important he was to her. She had no illusions that he felt the same. She only knew she wanted whatever time with him she could beg, borrow or steal. Maguire at his worst challenged her heart more than any man ever had.

Carolina didn't expect to see Maguire at his worst quite so soon, but walking into the hotel turned into an *eek*. A half-dozen messages were waiting for him, all marked Urgent. The hotel rooms he'd wanted weren't ready. Nothing was right.

Maguire didn't do frazzled, of course, he just went into hypermanagement mode. She was given a temporary room, with a couple hours free to nap and change clothes before they met in the lobby for dinner. He took over an office somewhere. It all worked out.

Actually, it more than worked out. Four hours later she was seated in a magical place. The restaurant had the look of a castle, washed in glowing gilt as the sun went down. They ate outside, their table on the veranda with the bay just below. From the white tablecloths to the sparkle of crystal, the atmosphere was elegant. Tables filled up, but conversations were muted, with others—mostly couples—enjoying the sights and sounds and smells of the fabulous scenery, fabulous meal. Carolina had never before seen more jewels in one spot. There were enough dazzling diamonds to cause neck and earaches.

Maguire, though, was his usual common-sense self. "You're certain you want to mix that Japanese sushi and the Thai curry?"

"I think the chances of my ever coming here again are nonexistent, so I'm trying everything they'll let me." She tried to keep her eyes off him. His business glitches had been taken care of, and he'd lost the take-charge posture, even looked relaxed. But he still stunned her in the tux.

Apparently tuxes were standard Monaco attire, judging from the number of men wearing them—but it was only Maguire who glued her attention. The shock-white shirt and formal black tux did something to him. He looked all brash and blond. A rogue trapped in gentleman's clothes. There was something not quite civilized in the tilt of his chin, the way he walked, the arch of his brow.

She'd had a blast dressing for dinner, but it wasn't as if she could compete with this crowd. Maguire had had Henry pack a few of her own clothes before this trip, but she was still limited in what she could pull together. The black satin pants and top had been on sale at T.J. Maxx the holiday before, and just happened to go perfectly with her red Versace shoes. Maybe the cowl neck could have used jewelry, but she didn't have anything for this sort of occasion or place, so her neck and wrists were bare. She'd stroked in some mousse to add body to her hair, used a simple crystal clip to make the style look more formal, but there was a limit to what she could do with the equipment she had.

Trying to impress Maguire wasn't a goal, anyway. Or trying to pretend she was something she wasn't. As far as Carolina could tell, trying to outthink Maguire was a waste of time. He didn't respect people who lied to him or tried to manipulate him.

So, she didn't have to do anything but be herself—a T.J. Maxx girl who intended to try everything on the menu—if they let her. The waiter, so far, had been a hundred percent on her side. "When I saw the menu didn't have any prices listed, I knew it had to be over the top. And since I'm on major greedy mode, how about if I pay for my own dinner?"

"Nice try. Not going to happen."

"Have you ever been here before?"

"To Monaco, once. But not to this restaurant. It's got a reputation around the world for being stupendous."

"It sure is." Midway through the meal, though, Maguire responded to the vibrator mode on his cell.

He stood up, apologized and moved away from the other diners to take the call. It was business, Carolina could tell, because he immediately went on hard-face mode. He listened. Spoke crisply. He hadn't told her what business glitches he'd been dealing with that afternoon—she suspected he never would. But whoever he was talking to, Carolina was mighty glad it wasn't her.

The interruption gave her a chance to stand up. She wasn't sure how many courses they'd finished—surely six or seven—and she was comfortably stuffed. She carried her half-filled wineglass to the balcony edge. Night had dropped. Clouds skimmed past necklaces of stars, and the turquoise waters of the Côte had turned black satin. Just below, cars kept delivering patrons to the restaurant....car models she'd never seen before anywhere.

She must have been there several minutes before she realized Maguire had joined her, and was leaning over the edge as she was. "You see down there...the first car, the one everyone's looking it? It's a Bugatti Veyron," he informed her. "It's the most expensive car in the world, if I remember right. Under two million, but not by much. It's the only car that can hit four hundred miles an hour."

"Where on earth could you drive four hundred miles an hour?"

"That's not the point."

She motioned below. "What's the yellow one?"

"Porsche 9ll. This year's model. Right behind him is a red car… It's one of the newest Ferraris. You can buy that one for a cool million. Oh. Man."

She glanced below, at the car that had finally brought Maguire to his knees. He wasn't drooling, but his tongue was all but hanging out. All she saw was a grayish car that looked like a long bug.

"The Pagani Zonda," he identified it. "She can go from zero to sixty miles per hour in 3.2 seconds. I had a chance to drive one a few months ago. An idiot friend of mine bought one. Drove it to my place just to show it off, wanted to make me suffer."

"Did you? Suffer appropriately?"

"Oh, yeah. Believe me, she's a honey. She could park in my driveway any time."

Finally, a chink in his armor. Carolina was charmed. "So…were you tempted to buy one?"

"Well…no. She's wonderful. But she's not exactly a car you could take for a trek in the mountains, much less drive in a snowstorm."

"Was it bad news?" she asked.

"Pardon?"

"All those business calls this afternoon and then, just now. You looked…annoyed."

"No. It was just some problems. Solving problems is what I do." He straightened. "And right now we have a problem to solve together—which is to find out how you take to gambling."

"That's easy. I can tell you right now, I'm a wild gambler."

"I'll have to see that to believe it."

"I'll stake both of us, since you sprang for dinner," she offered.

"I'll stake myself, Carolina….but I'm all for you using your own money to play with. My thought would be to give you a little stake to get you started, until you learn what the games are about."

"No way. I'm thrilled we're doing this. But I'll learn on my own money. Period."

He shot her a look. "Whew. You're getting tougher all the time."

She was used to his teasing, but this time it itched. Just because she'd been through a stretch when she was overwhelmed didn't mean she had no character or strength or skills. Just once, she'd like Maguire to see that she didn't need or want to be treated like Waterford crystal.

By the time they reached the infamous casino, she was buzzed. Maguire cupped her elbow as he escorted her past fountains and lights, and into the heart of the casino. The buzzed sensation intensified, just from the warmth of his hand on her arm. From the way he walked next to her, as if they were a couple. From the way her pulse did musical scales—in several pitches—just from being this close.

"So…do you have any ideas which games you'd like to play? Or like to learn?"

"Hey, I can hold my own at a card table. Trust me."

"I do trust you. The way I'd trust a lamb at a slaughterhouse. If you just wait here for a minute, I'll get us some chips. You pick the game—anything you want is fine by me."

"Baccarat," she voted.

"Yeah, I watched that James Bond movie when I was a kid, too. You tired?" he asked swiftly when she stumbled.

"No!" It was possible, very unlikely, but possible, that she'd been wearing her new shoes nonstop for a little too long and her feet were a wee bit tired. But admit that to Maguire, and she'd never hear the end of it. "I'll just wander around while you're getting the chips, okay?"

"Sure, but stay in sight. This is safer than an alley in a big city, but there are still sharks here. They just look nicer. I want you to have fun—but we're not putting you in any situations where you have to worry."

She couldn't have been less worried. She picked a baccarat table, and wedged herself between a woman draped in sapphires and a white-tuxed Japanese gentleman. There were no seats together, but Maguire had a spot at the end. The gaming table was one of the most crowded. The dealer, Carolina thought, spent more money on a hairstylist than she did. Was cuter, too.

She settled down on the velvet bar stool, not just prepared to have some fun playing the game, but to prove to Maguire that she wasn't such a sissy or a wuss. Granted, he'd seen her in bad shape, but that was before. Days ago. Aeons ago.

It seemed as if a lifetime had passed since she'd known Maguire. There'd been life before she met him. And life since. And "life since" was all that seemed to matter.

The dealer shuffled, dealt. Maguire's eyes met hers across the table. "The noise level bothering you?" he mouthed.

She shook her head, amazed at her own answer. Of course, all the casino noises were friendly, not scary. But it was only a couple weeks ago when she'd shrank from all noise. It was amazing to her—how much had changed. How much she'd changed.

The dealer dealt her a natural five—a potentially great card. She glanced at the chips Maguire had given her, and abruptly realized that her smallest chip was fifty dollars.

She almost had a heart attack. Got over it. And carefully bid a single chip.

Maguire picked up a face card in the deal, which in this game was the same as a zero. Still, anything could come through with the second card.

Carolina waited her turn. When the dealer sent her a second card, she shrieked—delicately—to reveal it was a four, making her two cards a natural baccarat. The dealer chuckled at her enthusiasm and paid her chips.

Twenty minutes later, Maguire burst onto the balcony with a grim face and alarmed eyes. "My God. Where have you been?"

"Just here. Enjoying the night." She could see how worried he looked. "Hey, I'm sorry. I was trying to give you some space so you could play. And I was happy enough, just enjoying the sights and sounds from the balcony here—"

"But you just won. Why'd you tear off?"

"Because I won."

"Huh? You won one hand."

"Well, yeah." She cocked her head, unsure what he was driving at. "I just made five hundred bucks on a single hand, Maguire. Why on earth would I bet again and risk losing that?"

He scooped an arm around her shoulders and shook his head. "C'mere, big gambler. I'll buy you one more glass of wine before we pack it in."

"I'll buy! I'm the rich one tonight, remember!"

Oh, that smile, she thought. The hint of whiskers

on his chin just made him look more roguish. He came through with the wine, and they both leaned back, inhaling the lights and warm night. "I saw another Porsche," she told him. "Yellow like a banana. Or maybe like a yellow submarine."

It was getting easier to woo smiles from him. Easier to get him to talk, let go a little. Eventually they wandered from the lighthearted to the more serious.

"You know what? I was thinking," she murmured.

"Women shouldn't do that. Men always get in trouble when that happens."

"Oh, good. You're scared." She leaned against the balcony, felt the cool concrete against her thighs, felt the sparkle of moonlight and fairy dust from this magical place. From being with him. Here. Just the two of them. "Brace yourself."

"Okay, I'm braced. Tell me what's on your mind."

"I've been working with special kids for quite a while. I love it. I love them."

"Is this the scary part? Because I'm pretty sure I already knew this."

"I'm getting to the scary part. Sheesh. Give me a chance. So. I've worked in two schools and four different summer programs. The job I had this last year was the best, but you know what?"

"I'll bite. What?"

"Maguire…I can tell you why people didn't notice what was wrong with Tommy. People in my field are programmed, we're trained, to work with the problems that we understand the children to have. Most of the classes are understaffed and underfunded—but that's not the whole problem. Money never is."

"Money never is? How can you be an American and think money isn't the solution to every problem? But go on. I have to hear where you're going with this."

"Well…this is the thing. We have some great programs for special kids. But we also miss things because we have to be concerned with the diagnosis of what's wrong. No child totally fits a pattern. Even a child with limited IQ can have spots when he's brilliant. Even a child with a definite diagnosis can have other sides to his health, his character, that aren't defined by what's wrong with him. I'd like to take that to D.C."

"Okay. Now you're starting to scare me."

"Oh, I realize I don't have the power to do anything myself. But…I do have money now. I could bring some of the best minds together on my dollar. Look at the best of programs we have, how to work with the multiple dimensions of each child. Being an advocate for special kids… I could actually do that. With some money and some power. I could actually make a difference at a higher level than just an individual classroom."

Maguire shifted, straightened up. "All right. I admit it. I didn't dream you'd get here this fast. You're starting to get it, how you can carve out your own life, now, aren't you? You're revving your own engine. This is a good idea."

"I'm a smart girl, Maguire. You doubted I would come up with good ideas?"

"I never doubted you were smart. I worried that the piranhas out there had beaten you down." He reached out a hand.

She took it.

"Ready to head back to the hotel? We've had a long day."

They had, but her heart was suddenly thrumming to bluesy rhythms. Maguire might not know it, but his evening wasn't completely over yet.

Chapter Seven

Back at the hotel, an open-gated elevator sent them to the third floor. Maguire could see that she was beat. He'd wanted her to have that kind of whirlwind day—so busy she didn't have time to dwell on fears or worries, but not so crazy that she'd get over-exhausted.

This hotel, like others in Monaco, went over the top on gilt and opulence. Not Maguire's choice of decors, but he'd be looking for the kind of place where Carolina'd feel pampered. The screw-up earlier in the day had been corrected. He plucked her key, 3543, opened her door and stepped in a foot, just to make sure the setup was correct.

The peach satin spread was turned down, a spray of Russian chocolates on the pillow, a dressing gown laid out. A light in the bathroom gleamed on the marble floor; soft lamplight pooled a welcoming glow by her bed. Two dozen peach roses spilled from an ivory vase. A basket of goodies—wine, cheese, fruit, snacks—was tucked on the far table.

Yes. All as ordered. Maguire backed out a step. "Okay, you. To sleep—for as long as you want to sleep. I'm in the next room, 3544."

Carolina raised her eyebrows. "You're not in a suite with me this time?"

Maguire had gotten smarter in direct proportion to her becoming more dangerous. "I'm right next door, and there's a connecting door between us that's locked on both sides. If you need me, I'm a knock away. But I don't think you need anyone hovering close the way I was before."

"You do think I'm stronger," she said with a tone of satisfaction.

"I do. But you don't need setbacks." And he didn't need to be any closer to that lithe body draped in black that clung in all the right places whenever she moved. "When you're ready to be out and about to-morrow, just knock on the connecting door. I brought work with me that I can do right in the room, so if you want to sleep all day, it won't matter to me. If you want to get up and moving, that's fine, too."

"That's it?" she murmured. "No kiss good-night, Maguire?"

He saw the look in her eyes. Had to bolster a breath before coming through with a teasing, "Hey. Behave yourself."

He let himself into his room, clunked down the key and kicked off his shoes. His mind was chanting mantras. Vanilla. Snow. Milk. Anything he could think of that would remind him of virgin white.

Carolina had formed…an attachment for him. He knew it. He refused to ignore it any longer. But she was vulnerable as satin, good from the inside out.

He'd been tainted from the day he was born.

He'd been in a position to rescue her, to steal her away to a princess life for a few days. Maguire got it. It was easy for her to see him as a knight in shining armor. But he was no knight. And he wasn't—and couldn't be—a serious part of her life long term. So it was up to him to make sure she didn't get hurt.

He yanked off the tux jacket, then the cumberbund and stupid tie. Bleach. Frost. Calcium. Pearls—no, not pearls, that texture and shade of white reminded him too much of her skin.

He needed white words that were, well, wilters. Nonsexual. Like…frost. Whitewash. Toothpaste. He undid his cuffs, then started on the shirt buttons.

Abruptly he heard the knock on the connecting door.

He went over, and unlocked his side. "What? Are you sick or…?"

His voice dropped when he saw her. She'd slipped off the black pants and top. Pulled on a satin nightgown in peach and lace. Her feet were bare, her makeup washed off, and the expression in her eyes was a hundred percent ticked off.

"You said I could have what I wanted. That I needed to be strong enough to stand up for what I wanted. Well, damn it, Maguire. I want my goodnight kiss and I want it now."

Okay. She was cute. But he could turn on the tough button any time he needed to, could get as heartless as he needed to be, any time.

At least usually.

The damn woman.

She stepped up, stepped in, clutched his open shirt in her small fists and took. Her lips trembled, even as they pressed. Her hands were coward-cold. And the swishy lingerie was killer-sexy, but she was ironed-tight against him as if fearing he might actually see any of that soft, vulnerable flesh.

He told himself to think about snow, damn it. Calcium. Milk. All those pure white turnoffs. All those reminders that Carolina was confused, very unsure what she wanted or needed right now.

Only…her hands dropped to his hips. She brazenly palmed his butt, nesting him closer to her. Naturally, his body responded as if prodded by a firecracker. That was her, the firecracker, with the little hot fingers and the little hot tongue.

That tongue slipped between his teeth, found his tongue, retreated. Came back for more. She made a sound, a groan like a she-cat, then rubbed her breasts against his chest as if they were itchy and rubbing against him was the only cure for easing that itch.

White, he told himself firmly.

And then, *Think white, Maguire.*

She didn't seem aware that winding herself around him invariably threw them both off balance. There was a moment when they both would have fallen—if he didn't reach out to steady her. That's all he did. Put his hands on her arms. Only for that millisecond. But even though he was chanting "white" at the top volume of his conscience...

Armageddon followed.

"Okay." He tore out a breath. "Okay, now. Carolina, listen to me—"

"No." That was all she said. No. And then she pushed him. Backward. Into his bedroom. His setup was similar to hers, maybe navy blue instead of feminine colors, but the same king-size bed, side couch and chair, all the usual suspects of an ultraluxurious hotel room.

She didn't look or care, as if whether she fell against chair legs or table sides was completely beneath her notice right then. Pushing him. That's all she was into. And when the back of his knees located the bed, she gave him one more little push and then tumbled on top of him, straddling him, leaning over with closed eyes to find his mouth again.

He had to get a grip. Get control. A man like him wasn't seduced. Ever. Didn't relinquish complete control with anyone. Ever. And that maxim was a mighty *never* where Carolina was concerned. So that was why he put his hands on her again.

It wasn't to sweep her beneath him. It was to stop her, from rubbing against his crotch, from dancing her satined body in the opening of his tux shirt, from breathing in her scent, her tongue, the desire beading off her in torrents.

Only, something went wrong.

He intended to push her away. He was outstanding at pushing people away, had his whole life, only somehow… Magic? Miracles? Bad luck? She seemed to twist at just the wrong time, so that he ended up on top of her. And once she was beneath him, her slim legs rose up and high, clasping around his hips, inviting him in, teasing him closer, closer. She arched her back, so the brush of her breasts could cause him more torment. Her skin heated. Her damn mouth started trembling again. She made that earthy little wicked groan again.

Finally, from the scrabbled, scrambled contents

of his brain came some words. "Okay. Okay. This is okay. For a few minutes. Nothing wrong…"

"You're darned right there's nothing wrong. This is as right as anything I can ever remember."

"Just because…this is a little unexpected…doesn't mean we've done anything…unforgivable…"

"Yet," she qualified, and ruthlessly took a nip from his neck.

"Yet? Yet?"

"I'm about to do something unforgivable," she promised him. "With you. Only with you."

"Now, Carolina—"

"I don't care if you respect me in the morning."

"Now, Carolina—"

"What? You think the whole world's going to crash if you take off the good-guy hat for a whole ten minutes? Or is it that you need an engraved invitation?"

He didn't need an invitation. He needed something, someone, somehow to knock some sense into his head, but once she said "ten minutes," he lost it. What little brain he had left. Ten minutes? That's all she thought it'd take to be made love to? Made love with?

Hell, she might as well have tossed a red scarf at a bull.

The slightest shift and tug, and he was enabled to

remove that delectable, fragile slip of satin off her skin, and then he had her naked.

His senses both blurred and sharpened. He expected the peaches and ivory…not the sizzling heat and impatience. He expected the same-as-innocent… but not the brazen-I-own-you-Maguire bravado.

That was the whole problem. She touched, she stroked, she kissed, as if she owned. As if this moment was her inarguable right, to claim, to master. To *feel*. Everything. With him.

You just didn't walk into forest fires. Everybody knew that, coming straight out of the womb…except for her. She needed tenderness, yet demanded rough speed and roller-coaster tension. She bruised too damn easily, yet she bit and kneaded and pulled, with her mouth, with her hands, in a fight for…he didn't know what the hell she was fighting for.

He just knew that he wanted to fight with her. For her. His skin turned slick, his blood thick. The shine in her eyes was so fierce, so greedy. Any hesitation or caution on his part, she met with whispered dares. Real dares. Crazy, crazy dares. Like…to walk on moonlight with her. To dance on honey. To sing with their fingers. See? How impossibly crazy and silly she was? How life-young?

It was all total foolishness. Except…

Except…

That he couldn't remember, ever, having the chance to be foolish.

Couldn't remember, ever, letting his guard down, because he knew, he *knew,* how sharply a man could get hurt. How jagged a wound could be. How deeply a man could be scarred. If he didn't protect himself.

He just didn't know how to protect himself with her.

Carolina fell asleep, but only for a short time. She didn't want to sleep. She'd had enough rest for aeons. In some ways, she was discovering she'd been asleep her whole life.

And looking at Maguire was a heady way to enjoy staying awake. At first moonlight flooded in the balcony doors, making his skin look silver, the wild thrash of his hair making shadows on the far wall. His face, in repose, was the strong marble of statues, the whole Greek god thing.

After moonlight came that long, dark stretch, where she could barely see him, even the shadow of him…but she could hear his deep, quiet breathing. Feel the weight of his arm, his hand, when he tucked her close to him, almost inside of him…and how, even in sleep, he stroked. Soothed. Enticed.

Maguire was ultraskilled at locking up his emotions—when he was awake. He'd revealed so much, making love with her. She hadn't guessed before…

that Maguire was as vulnerable as she was. That he was risking as much as he was.

He'd been counseling her to go after what she wanted and needed—but had he ever done just that with his own life?

At least she'd risked opening her heart to people. Maybe too much. But Maguire was so, so alone.

Except for last night. She had no doubt at all about the love inside the man. The heart inside the man.

And now, after darkness came that predawn color, not gray, more like a slow seeping yellow, pearling the air, turning charcoal shadows back into inanimate things with color and life and depth. Dawn showed the stubble on Maguire's chin, the pleat of a sun-wrinkle around his eyes, the paintbrush-thick eyelashes. Even in the cool of the night, he hurled off the blankets and sheets. Somehow even in sleep, he'd kept her covered, but for himself, he kicked off any warmth—except for her. Out of nowhere, she'd find his arm sneaking around her again. Then his sigh of relief, as if finding her still there enabled him to go back to sleep again.

He slept nude. So did she. But he sure looked better in dawn light than she did. Which was when he suddenly opened his eyes and found her staring at him.

Maguire—her Maguire—wasn't a blusher. But a

little alarm seemed to shoot up his neck as if she'd caught him doing something…wicked.

Which of course she had.

"We didn't really do that," he said, his voice still night-thick.

"Oh yeah, we sure did. Twice, I believe."

A fingertip touched her cheek, his tenderness a direct contradiction to the sudden scowl ruffling his brow. "This wasn't in the game plan, Carolina."

"Well, feel free to wallow in guilt, if you want. I won't stop you. But you might want to consider that… well, maybe I needed this. To heal. Maybe I needed to be made love to, specifically by you. You can just think of it as part of the job. Part of the project you signed up for."

"You're not a job or a project, Carolina."

She shrugged. "I don't want to hear a bunch of integrity-and-responsibility stuff. I want breakfast. A decadent breakfast. A seven-cheese omelet, over-loaded with cholesterol, like real butter, and French toast, and fresh orange wedges…"

"Where are you going?"

She could see from his expression that he wanted a further serious morning-after discussion, so she slid out of bed. "The shower. My shower. While I do that, I'm hoping you'll order our decadent breakfast."

"We will be leaving the room for breakfast."

She didn't wince. Her brilliant smile didn't falter

either. But she got the message. He wasn't going to be alone with her if he could help it, not after last night.

He'd liked it, Maguire. Her. The sex. Being loved by her, with her. She didn't doubt that.

But he wanted her long term in his life like he wanted a sliver. He was here to fix her. That was all. To do the responsible thing and get her healed, before dropping her back in her real life and out of his hair again.

She got it, she got it.

But after last night, she was going to have a lot harder time pretending it was that simple for her again. Or ever could be.

Downstairs, one of the hotel restaurants served breakfast in the open patio overlooking the bay. The tables were dressed as elegantly as last night, with gleaming silver and crystal, accenting an impeccably perfect day. Guests milled everywhere, all ages, many looking glamorous and foreign, some dressed casually, fresh off their boats—or yachts, as it were.

Personally, Carolina thought she was appropriately dressed for a hot sunny morning, in a linen skort and shimmery-cool tank top and, of course, her red shoes. So did Maguire, judging from the way he kept looking at her.

But he kept her talking about serious issues as if the sky might fall if he let down his hair. There was no way he was stepping off the mentor role this morning. Even when he sipped the delectably tangy OJ. Bit into the lightest, softest, richest omelet ever made. Lingered on bites of toast dripping with hot, wild blueberries.

"So, we're going to talk about some of the things you want to do," he said.

"Yes, sir."

"Part of your stress load was so many people asking you constantly for things. Everyone in your life wanting something from you. So let's start with your parents. Are there some things you actually do want for them?"

"Oh, yes. Absolutely." She could love up Maguire with her eyes and still do this serious-talk stuff. She valued his advice and ideas, besides. "I want to make their lives easier. Give them security. I loved setting my mom up with a new kitchen, giving my dad the car of his dreams. I would have loved to give them treats like that forever…"

"But then it wasn't so easy. Instead of giving, they started having expectations. Until there seemed no end to the expectations."

When she reluctantly nodded, he went on. "So here's the deal, Cee. You want to give your parents security? Do it. Pay for great health insurance, if they don't already have it. Pay off their mortgage if you want. Then, set up a trust. Establish the trust to supplement their retirement income. And then that's it. You're done."

Reluctantly she leaned away from the plate. If she ate any more, she'd turn into a balloon...but damn, the food was good. "Only in theory, Maguire. Because that's what I was discovering. No matter what I do, it seems like it didn't stop them from asking for more—"

"I get that. Trust me. But what you have to get straight in your head is what you want to do for them, then do it. And then you draw the line in the sand. You need to know, in your heart, that what you set up is generous and fair and right. So you know, absolutely, there's no reason to feel guilty."

All right. Maybe she felt loverlike and cuddly and turned on. But nobody seemed to reach her like Maguire. This stuff mattered. She frowned. "That isn't how I'm used to thinking about things."

"Yeah, I know. You don't think 'selfish.' And you're a lousy student at learning selfishness, if you ask me."

"Hey! I'm plenty selfish! Look at the shoes!" She lifted a leg, just to illustrate.

"Okay, okay, I admit it. You did good on the shoes. But we have to work a little harder on your getting tougher with the rest of it."

"Like with what?"

"Well..." Maguire leaned forward, poured them

both fresh coffee from the carafe. "You said that your father wanted to handle your money."

Her stomach instantly knotted. "And his feelings were terribly hurt when I didn't leap to say yes. In fact, I cried—"

"Hey. No. No crying. Listen to me." For a second his voice almost took on a panicked tone. "Your father is no more capable of handling big money than you are. That isn't an insult. It's just a fact. Would you go to a plumber for brain surgery?"

"No."

"Repeat after me—No, of course not."

"No, of course not."

"Would you go to a brain surgeon to fix a leaky faucet?"

She knew her line. "No, of course not."

"Exactly. So you get people to help you with the money who are, so to speak, brain surgeons with money. Reputable brokers. Finance people with established reputations. If your dad can't understand that, he'll have to get over it. That's not on you. It'd be stupid to let the plumber to do the brain surgery, remember? You can't make your parents' lives easier if all that money goes down the drain because of poor management."

"Look, I'm getting sick and tired of your being right, Maguire. I'm starting to feel like a dunce."

"You're not a dunce. You're ultrabright. Just not

about big money. How could you be? And why should you expect yourself to be brilliant about everything? See…I'm way better at being selfish than you are. That's why I'm the natural teacher in this."

She opened her mouth to say something sassy and clever…it was about time she put him in his place. He was mighty comfortable in the role of 'Fixing Carolina.' Not so comfortable when she turned the tables and made him talk about himself.

She was about to direct a raft of questions at him… when a commotion across the patio diverted her attention. Although most of the tables were filled, most conversations were desultory, natural to guests enjoying a leisurely morning and fabulous food. But at the far table near the aqua pool, voices suddenly raised.

Carolina glanced over, and saw what looked to be a father and teenage daughter. Although they weren't fighting in English, she could easily get the gist. Likely similar arguments took place in every household on every continent, when a daughter was trying to grow up before her daddy thought she was ready.

Their voices kept rising. The daughter snapped back, sassy, from her tone. The father's retorts became colder, sterner. It was just an argument. Just a personal fight.

There was just a moment…when the blond-haired

girl stopped looking defiant and strong. She…caved. Whatever her dad said…hurt.

Crushed her. The lips trembled. The eyes welled. Her so-pretty face looked full of pain, beyond hurt.

Carolina could feel her pain. Could remember feeling as if she was breaking from all the people yelling at her, not hearing anything she said, until the words wounded beyond bearing. And just like that, she suddenly lost it. The sound of their voices. All their voices. All sound.

The stupid hysterical deafness was back. She shook her head, but it was like trying to shake water from her ears after swimming. Any sound that came through was just a pale blur, nothing with any decibels.

Maguire saw the change in her. She knew from his expression.

He couldn't know what triggered the problem this day—Carolina wasn't sure she could explain it to herself—but Maguire didn't need all the answers to act.

He just turned into her hero again. Anger steeled his expression—but not anger at her. He swept her up and out of there, an arm around her shoulder, steering her past people, past doors, past everything. Carolina sensed that he'd battle off a few armies if they tried getting near her.

He steered her through his room, to get to hers. Coaxed her to lie down. Put a warm cloth on her forehead. Came through with tea. And a foot rub. American newspapers to read.

She must have napped, because when she woke up, she found her red shoes on a pillow in her sight—a picture that was guaranteed to make her smile.

The short nap seemed to fix the hearing problem this time, because she could hear bursts of laughter and splashing from the pool below. Sweet sunlight pooled in the windows, and she heard Maguire's voice, quiet, talking on a phone from the balcony. He was using his "making arrangements" voice.

When he stopped talking, she assumed he'd finished the call, and spoke up. "So where are we going, Maguire?"

Faster than the spin of a dime, he charged in, studied her face with the fierceness of a scientist—not a lover. His stiff shoulders eased. "You're hearing again."

"Yup. And I'm sorry. Angry at myself. That was stupid. The whole deaf thing is stupid. I'm strong now."

"You are strong, Carolina. You're just not tough. There's a difference."

"I'm both." She swung her legs over the side of the bed, pushed a hand through her hair. "I've had it with this weakling business. So I had some stress. Everybody has stress. They don't just cave. I'm through being a wuss."

"You were never a wuss, Carolina."

Arguing with him was useless. She should have known. "I heard you making some kind of travel arrangements, or that's what it sounded like. So where are we going?"

A smile finally broke through that austere frown. "First, we've got a few hours before our flight. So… we're getting you another suitcase, and you've got two or three hours' worth of a shopping spree to fill it. After that…we're headed to one of the places on your list. And I'll admit, you gave me a real challenge coming through on this one. You're going to love it."

She didn't plan on loving anything. She'd found a lover last night—an unforgettable lover. But because she'd done the stupid hysterical-deafness thing again, he had a chance to push away. He had a great time doing his fix-Carolina thing…but no one was getting close enough to fix Maguire.

Truthfully she didn't want to fix anything about him. She just wanted to show him that someone could be there for him, too. That it wasn't always one-sided.

So far, she'd flunked that course completely.

Chapter Eight

Well, hell. Maguire fixed things. He was good at fixing things—not to be egotistical, but personally, he thought he was downright outstanding at fixing things.

But he was rotten when fate threw him a curveball that he wasn't prepared for.

"We're just going back to Washington for a couple of days," he told Carolina. The interminable overseas flight was…well, interminable.

"You told me. It's fine." Carolina, curled up in the window seat, looked sleepy and content.

Maguire wanted to claw the walls. "That wasn't the plan."

"I know. And I get it, you're stressed about this. But whatever you have to do, just do, Maguire. You told me Tommy was coming over tomorrow. I couldn't be more delighted to see him."

He could see she meant it. Her eyes lit up at the idea of seeing his young brother—so unlike the rest of the world, who looked at Tommy and tended to see disabilities.

The change in plans had a good side, he told himself. They were going to be around people for a couple of days, rather than alone together. She'd have a block of time to forget that wild night, to get things back in perspective. He'd keep her way, way too busy to think about...well, to think about sex. At least sex with him.

By the time the jet finally touched down in Seattle, they were both blithering tired. Maguire didn't usually suffer from jet lag, but he hadn't slept. How was he supposed to sleep, when the damn woman had put down the barrier between the seats and snuggled next to him?

She made out like his chest was her pillow. Like his arm belonged tucked around her. Like it was okay that her hand had drifted between his legs when she fell asleep. That her hand had been there for ages and ages. That the damn woman had reached up to brush her lips against his neck in her sleep, for Pete's sake.

Was that fair? Was that reasonable? How much could a man be expected to endure?

He'd arranged a limo to pick them up in Seattle, which saved him having to drive when he was bleary-eyed. Once they got back to the lodge, she poured into bed almost as easily as liquid Jell-O, only spoke up when he took off her sacred red shoes.

He had no memory of stumbling into bed, but he must have, and then woke up early in spite of himself. Maybe he was brain-dead tired, but he still figured the rise-and-shine thing was a good idea—he'd have a chance to mentally prepare before Carolina was up.

The rain started at dawn, beginning as a sleepy drizzle and turning into a silent gush. Even inside, the pines seemed to smell more verdant, the air steamed with freshness. By the time Carolina bounced downstairs, in jeans and an oversize sweatshirt, he had a table loaded with papers and information for her—and he was on the nice, far distance of the other side.

He poured her coffee, urged her to sit and started in. "I've got a list for you…"

He had a plan, beyond keeping her busy with coffee and thick slabs of French-bread toast. He was going to give her lots to do. Lots to think about. And no time to think of anything personal about him, or them, for damn sure.

"First, here's a list of good lawyers. Then another list of financial and bank people. Before going with any, you should interview them, talk to them, make sure you're comfortable communicating with them. It doesn't help to have smart, good people if they're speaking Russian to your French. And then…"

She made several hmm sounds, verifying that she was paying attention, listening. But she didn't stay sitting long. She got up, pressed a hand on his shoulder, started a fresh pot of coffee.

No one had told her where stuff was in the kitchen, but she seemed to guess that spoons would be in the drawer by the sink, mugs in the cupboard above. Maybe women were born knowing this stuff.

And maybe she'd forgotten about that other night, Maguire thought. It didn't seem possible, when the sex had been so earth-shattering. But she was walking around the kitchen, her hair a little tangled, her face with no makeup, barefoot, as if she didn't have a care in the world.

She opened a bottom cupboard in the pantry, found a box of brownie mix, lifted it to read the back.

Her fanny was probably the finest he'd ever seen. The sweatshirt completely concealed her figure, but that was the thing. She moved, with that light lithe grace, and there it was—a hint of her breast when she turned, the curve of her hip when she bent down.

Promise. Every damn thing about the woman was a capital *P* promise.

For the right man.

Not him.

But for the right one.

"Every time I've seen you lose your hearing, Carolina, it's clearly because you hit a stressor. The last couple of times, it seems the stress trigger was seeing someone emotionally hurt, or feeling beat up on, or being yelled at. So that's what we're working on next. We're going to set up life situations where no one can do that to you."

"Do you like your brownies with nuts or not?"

"I like homemade brownies any way I can get them. Are you listening?"

"Yes, sir." Another squeeze on his shoulder, just a whisper of contact, but by the time he whipped around, she was fussing around the kitchen again.

So he started talking faster. "One of the things you've been clear about is wanting to share your wealth. Wanting to use some of your money to just plain give away—"

"Darned right I do." Just for a second, there was a flash of fire in those soft blue eyes. "There are so many causes and people with huge needs."

"I know, buttercup." The stupid "buttercup" word just slipped out, but Maguire stayed firmly on course. "That's exactly the point. You need a way to handle that, where people aren't battering down your door all the time. So here's what you do. Decide how much you want to give away to worthy causes in a year. Put that money into a type of account or trust. Then hire someone—part-time, you can make it a single mom or someone who needs to work from home, so you'll get to do your do-gooder thing that way, too. That in-between person hears all the direct requests, studies the causes, then reports to you—you and you alone decide which ones to give to. But you're able to stay separate from the people making demands of you. No hounders get to you directly. So…"

He'd been lecturing great guns, until she suddenly turned around. She'd been pouring the brownie mix into a pan, was still scraping the bowl with a spoon. But she had chocolate—just a tear—on her cheek.

She walked over, with that dripping spoon and the chocolate kiss on her cheek, and kissed him on the forehead. Just like that. Got chocolate on his brow. On his knee. She didn't even notice.

Hell. He didn't either.

"Maguire," she said gently, "I'm not telling you often enough how much I appreciate all this. You're teaching me tons. Giving me ideas I would never have had without you. You really get it. That I wasn't doing a good job of protecting myself. That I didn't know how. But I keep wondering…"

"What?" His tone came out snappy for no reason at all.

"Do you ever let anyone protect you?"

The question was ridiculous. Why would he need protecting from anyone or anything? He didn't know what she was getting at, only that she was increasingly starting to…worry him. He felt like a cat in a thunderstorm who couldn't sit still, just wanted to restlessly prowl and snap and worry.

She was messing with his head. He just wasn't sure how. Thankfully the strange moment ended abruptly with several exuberant knocks on the front door. Seconds later, Henry—looking beleaguered—piled in along with Tommy, Maguire's ex-sister-in-law, Shannon, and Tommy's dog. The dog was named Woofer, a disreputable cross between a St. Bernard and a Newfoundland—which meant that it stood table high, shed hair in buckets every hour, produced ropes of drool, and weighed in somewhere around two hundred pounds.

Tommy and Woofer both galloped straight for Carolina. "Miss Cee! It's *me! Tommy!*"

"I can see that! I'm so excited to see you again!" As if she was used to horse-size dogs, she gave Woofer a kiss and Tommy a monster-size hug. The dog aimed promptly for the brownie mix, which Carolina swooped out of reach just in time. The pan went in the oven, and Carolina settled on the floor with Tommy, the dog, and quickly abandoned jacket and gloves and shoes. "I think you've grown a foot since last summer."

"I did! Everybody says. Miss Cee. Do you remember saving my life?"

"I remember being in that big noisy ambulance with you."

"I remember that, too!"

"I remember your telling me that you didn't like doctors. Or shots. And I don't either. So it's a good thing we could do that together, huh?"

"Yeah. I remember that whole day."

"Me, too."

Henry gave a shudder as he passed the dog, honed in on the coffeemaker, filled a mug and retreated to the library, as far away from dog hair and confusion as he could get.

Maguire's ex-sister-in-law beelined straight for him. "I'm glad you could spare the time," Shannon said.

Since Shannon only called him about problems with Tommy—and she knew he'd move heaven and earth for his brother—she had no reason to be surprised. He didn't like interrupting his plans with Carolina, but there was no answer he could have given except "of course."

Shannon was one of the few things his older brother had done right—and divorcing Jay was one of the things Shannon had done right as well. She looked like an expensive socialite, from the crown of her red head to her designer socks—but she had heart. Staying with Jay any longer could well have killed it. And although she liked living high—which caretaking Tommy enabled her to do—she'd loved the boy from the start and vice versa. "He really wanted to see her," Shannon said, referring to Carolina. "But I sure didn't expect this."

Neither did Maguire. Tommy hung back from people outside his household. Especially in the last few years he'd become aware that he didn't talk "right," so in public he tended to keep silent, not wanting others to realize he was different.

With Carolina, he turned into a babbling brook. When he was excited, his speech became more incoherent, but Carolina just slowed the pace of her own conversation, and seemed to understand his excited gibberish just fine.

Tommy had grown ten inches since the summer before, was taller than Carolina now, looked like a normal all-American kid of twelve. His blond hair was styled with cowlicks. He was all arms and legs, with huge blue eyes and a smile that'd win over anyone, anything, any time.

Maguire had known for a long time that he could kill anyone who hurt his vulnerable brother, but he'd never met anyone who related to him as naturally as Carolina.

Shannon said, "I can't believe it. She's just great with him."

In spite of the chilly, rainy afternoon, Tommy wanted to run around outside—with Carolina and Woofer. Maguire thought the idea was insane, but he had business issues to discuss with Shannon, the more private the better.

They both stood at the window, watching Carolina and Tommy in the yard.

"Wow," Shannon murmured again. "You know what? From what I'd heard about her, she's exactly what I expected."

"And what did you expect?"

"A sweetie. A do-gooder teacher. Someone softer than a pansy, real good with kids, nothing cynical or jaded about her." Shannon pivoted on a high-heeled boot. "Which makes her the last woman in the universe I expected you to fall for."

"That's a pretty amazing conclusion to reach, considering you just met her two seconds ago."

Shannon smelled the brownies, marched over to give them a peek, then reached for a hot pad and pulled the pan out to the stovetop. "There's nothing wrong with falling, Maguire. It happens to the best of us. I guess I just expected you to fall for…I don't know…a grad from a fancy East Coast school, maybe a pissy lawyer in stilettos, the kind of woman who'd been breaking glass ceilings from the get-go."

He didn't answer. As fond as he was of Shannon—and he was—he didn't talk about his personal life, with her or anyone else. If and when he got around to marrying, he might have envisioned someone like she'd described. But that was a totally different issue than…falling.

"I'm not sure I really see a need for marriage."

"You never saw a need for people putting themselves in a trap where they're likely to strangle each other and cause lasting scars," Shannon retorted.

"Yeah. Isn't that what I just said?" Truthfully, he'd always wanted kids. He just never bought into the fairy tale. If children came into the picture, he expected to marry, expected to be a damn good partner, faithful, supportive, that whole experience. He just never wanted to put love in that frame. He'd grown up seeing exactly what "love" could do, how twisted a relationship could become because of money. It never even entered his mind as an option.

"Maguire." Shannon stood inches from the brownies as if they'd cool faster if she hovered that close. "It's in your face. The way you look at her. I've never seen you before—"

He cut her off. "We really don't have time for chitchat. Carolina and Tommy'll be back any minute. When you called, you said there was a financial crisis."

She looked away. "I'm afraid you'll yell at me."

"Have I ever yelled at you? Even once?"

"No, but…"

"Just get it said. We'll deal with it." Maguire suspected he didn't really need to hear the story. The refrain was always the same.

When their father died, Jay had gotten primary custody of Tommy for two reasons—one was that he was the eldest son, and second, because he'd asked his father for it. Jay had wanted the living allowance set up for Tommy in his own pocket….but Jay had never really wanted to give his brother time or attention.

Shannon was no relationship to any of them, but she'd loved Tommy from the day he was born, and Tommy revered her. So she'd taken on the maternal role, by her choice—by everyone's choice. Maguire had guaranteed a generous allowance to maintain his brother's housing and welfare in every way, knowing that Jay would run through Tommy's money faster than a forest fire.

And that was exactly the problem. Jay was forever overspending his trust, and every time, he'd hit up Shannon. He always had the ace card, because he'd threaten to withdraw Tommy from her care if she didn't fork over the money.

It was the same story this time. The whole thing

made Maguire tired. Yeah, of course he immediately stepped in to solve the problem, but the situation underlined why he needed to stop thinking about Carolina in a personal way. Money didn't change anything that mattered. Life was ugly—at least his life was. Money invariably provoked selfishness and greed—and gave power to those who shouldn't have it. It wasn't a life he'd want for Carolina.

It was a life he'd be embarrassed to share, particularly with someone as good as she was.

"Well," Shannon suddenly murmured. "Will you look at what the cat dragged in."

He'd already turned his head at the sounds of commotion in the doorway. Carolina, Tommy, and the dog poured through the door, laughing, spraying water like puppies, everybody muddy. "We had a tiny fall," Carolina called out.

"Yeah. We slid down this long hill!" Tommy said exuberantly.

"Only there was this puddle—"

"Except the puddle turned out big as a lake!"

Carolina held up her hands. "Nobody worry! We'll fix this! We're headed straight for showers. Um, Maguire, where's the washing machine?"

"For you or the dog?"

And yeah, he was laughing. But the sound of laughter in his heart was bittersweet. Mud or no mud, Carolina was pure clean from the inside and out, nothing ugly tainting her life—the way a whole lot of wrong things irrevocably colored his.

By evening, the unflappable Maguire seemed to be in a downright snarly mood. Carolina could see he'd had a great time with Tommy, and the boy loved every minute with his older brother. She liked Tommy's caretaker, Shannon, even if she hadn't quite grasped how an ex-wife of Tommy's brother—someone who wasn't remotely blood kin—had gotten the parenting job. It didn't really matter. It was obvious the boy was thriving under Shannon's care.

When Shannon and Tommy—and the behemoth dog—left after dinner, Maguire's pretend-upbeat posture sagged. He disappeared in the library for a while. She had dinner with Henry, who groveled for more brownies, and urged her to have patience with Maguire.

There was nothing to have patience about. He was just…unhappy about something, unsettled. He spoke to her, spoke to Henry, had dinner, said the right things. It was in his eyes that something was wrong.

He'd closed up like a clam in a storm.

Both of them still had jet lag. When his eyes closed, watching the news, Carolina thought maybe exhaustion was the only thing going on, and heaven knew, she crashed soon after.

The morning brought sunshine—and an extraordinary surprise out the back door. When she looked out, she found Maguire and Henry both outside, even at this early hour, holding coffee and circling the surprise like lions guarding a hunt.

As fast as she could pile on clothes, she chased downstairs and outside, shrieking all the way, leaving the door open and not wasting time on a coat, no matter what the temperature.

It was a joke. Her asking for a ride in a '53 MG. Something on that silly list she'd made when she first came—it seemed like years ago—nothing that she remembered or ever expected to be taken seriously.

The baby was candy-apple-red, with fat fenders over her front wheels, a running board, a front hood that gleamed like a mirror. She'd only seen one once before. Didn't know what a Mark IV was from a TD or any other label like that…she'd just sat in the one car that her grandfather had worked with, and fell in love.

Both men turned at the sound of her screams, and for the first time in a solid twenty-four, she caught Maguire's real grin. He opened the bitsy door, motioned her inside into the old, black leather seat.

"Where did you guys *find* this?"

"Don't ask. Just next time, ask for world peace, or something that's easy to come by."

Henry started tsk-tsking at her bare feet and lack

of coat, being the fastidious old mother hen that he was, but the car was so one-of-a-kind adorable. Only after another few minutes oohing and aahing did she notice the duffel bag in back.

"We're going to be gone for twenty-four hours. Not far. Not sure how far we can trust the car—but Henry'll be here, home, ready to send out the Mounties if she's not in the mood to run well."

"You mean I can actually *drive* it?"

"I don't know," Maguire murmured. "Can you? I mean, I'll be glad to take the wheel if you're afraid of it—"

"But I can?"

Maguire spun a circle as if searching everywhere in sight. "Do you see anyone stopping her, Henry? Of course, maybe we should have crash helmets before letting her behind the wheel. And a quick course in what a clutch is for—"

"I grew up on jalopies, Maguire. I know what a clutch is. My grandpa used to restore old cars."

"So that's how you knew about this baby?"

"Yeah. He found and fixed up an old MG for a neighbor." She could see both he and Harry were in lust. They should look at women the way they looked at the car. They stroked. Drooled. Looked with reverence. Praised every body part. Revered.

Which gave her plenty of time to yank on clothes

and shoes and a jacket and run back outside. Maguire was already installed in the passenger seat.

"I thought maybe you'd let me drive," he said.

"Maybe in the next life. This was my fantasy. Not yours."

"But I didn't know about this car until you brought it up."

"Not my problem." She sank into the old leather, savoring the adorable dash, the tiny wheel, the long sleek front.

"What happened to my frugal, unselfish, can't-accept-anything-for-herself woman I met a week ago?"

"You ruined her, Maguire. Until you, I had no idea being corrupted could be so much fun. Snap on your seat belt. Oh. There are no seat belts. Then just hold on and pray, big boy, while we see what she can do."

She hadn't forgotten Maguire's moodiness the day before. He hadn't, of course, mentioned that anything was troubling him, because Maguire wouldn't. Not to her. Not to anyone, as far as she could tell.

Carolina was increasingly aware that her place in Maguire's life had been carefully, completely, sharply defined by him. Once she was "better," as he called it, he had every intention of disappearing—back to his life, whatever he did, whoever he did it with. If she felt something more, it was her problem. She'd cracked his armor when they made love, but he hadn't willingly opened his heart to her. Even an inch.

Possibly that was why she made the first turn on two wheels. She didn't want to give Maguire a heart attack exactly. More like an attack of the heart.

Within two miles, she'd mastered the four gears and aimed for some nice, steep, curly mountain roads.

"Does the phrase 'oh, my God' make you think we should slow down a little?" he asked over the wind.

"Nope."

"Hey. Where is my shy, softhearted school-teacher?"

"That was then. This is now." She had to shout to be heard above the wind. "Maybe you don't find out what a girl's made of until she has the chance to get behind the wheel, Maguire." She glanced at him, but only a millisecond of a glance. The steep road had no guardrails, every swinging turn and swerve creating blind spots. Like falling in love with him, she thought. There were unknown dangers behind every turn. Reckless dangers. Worrisome dangers. But damned if her heart wasn't racing with the thrill of it.

"Carolina." He was white-knuckled, holding the dash and door. Laughing. But definitely holding on. "Do you think there's a prayer we could return the car in one piece?"

The car, yes, she thought.

But her heart had already been cracked, hard.

And if streaking mountain roads at breakneck speed was what it took to make him laugh, she wasn't about to put her sensible shoes back on now.

Whatever time she had left with him, she was determined to give it everything she had.

Chapter Nine

It took enormous motivation to get her to park the car, but then, Maguire prided himself at being able to occasionally achieve the impossible.

She started yelling at the top of her lungs.

While she was occupied, Maguire crawled out of the old MG and kissed the cold, damp ground. He was that grateful to be alive. He wanted to give himself credit—Carolina most distinctly was not depressed or despondent, the way he'd first found her. The sound of her shrieks was damn well worth gold. And he was going to enjoy them. After kissing the ground. He hadn't been sure she was even listening to his directions, much less following them. The last ten minutes he'd been praying with his eyes closed.

"Maguire! Quit that! You weren't that terrorized by my driving!"

"Oh, yes, I was," he said feelingly, in no hurry to get off his knees.

He hadn't been afraid of anything since he could remember, but he was starting to be mighty afraid of Carolina. She was doing just what he wanted her to do—becoming strong, becoming happy, standing up for herself more and more. It was just…

She wasn't predictable. At least she wasn't predictable with him.

Her excited shrieks, though, were very, very Carolina. At least when Carolina was happy. So if other issues weren't perfect, Maguire was determined to be careful. To do the right thing. To finish up the fixing and healing of Carolina—no matter what it took.

"Maguire! How did you find this? I can't believe you found this! Oh, my heavens. I didn't even know anything like this existed! It was just a crazy fantasy idea, for heaven's sake!"

She charged over—he knew damn well to throw herself in his arms; she was that excited, that beside herself. So he swiftly got to his feet and pulled a duffel bag from the back of the car, staving off any contact between them. "You ready to climb up?" he asked her.

"Are you kidding?"

Some women fantasized about jewels and furs. She'd wanted to spend the night in a tree house. Finding the jewels would have been a whole lot easier, but Maguire had to admit, he'd outdone himself this time.

He'd seen pretty much everything, but this was as close to plain old simple fun. It was easy enough to find a tree house, just not an adult tree house, much less within reasonable driving distance. This one fit all the criteria.

He didn't know trees, but figured the base was one of the giant pines or spruces, because the top almost reached the sky. Midway up—thirty ladder steps up—a guy named McConnell had built an octagon-shaped cabin around the trunk. All the walls were tinted glass.

At the top of the ladder—he followed Carolina's butt—was a push-up door. Next to it was a pulley device intended to carry things up and down, such as the duffel Maguire had packed for the two of them, and the groceries Henry had boxed up.

The pulley was damn fun. While Carolina took off exploring, he brought the gear up and started stowing, feeling like a kid playing hooky. The only regular door in the place concealed a tiny bathroom and shower—it had glass windows like the rest of the tree house, but heaven knew, no one could see them at that height.

The architect had been intent on building green. The main living area was heated with a solar-powered heater. The minikitchen used solar power, as well, to chill, heat and store. A cupboard opened to reveal a pull-out collapsible table. A double-size beanbag functioned as a giant chair, big enough for two. A single bed—Maguire kept his eyes off it, as did Carolina—was double-sleeping-bag size, nothing fancy.

A small generator provided the possibility of electricity, but it was hard to imagine a need for TV or fancy music. The entertainment was all free. The view from the trees was more than magnificent. Stinging-fresh air, crusty hilltops and valleys, endless birds and wildlife below. Chocolate earth. Sharp greens. Diamonds in the sneaky curl of a creek below.

"I love you, Maguire," Carolina crowed.

His heart stopped for a second, but of course recovered. "Yeah, that's what all the girls say."

"You went above and beyond to find this place."

"I like the hero status, but I have to admit...I'm crazy about the place myself. You hungry? We just have picnic-type food. A lot of it, but nothing fancy."

They'd both skipped breakfast, though, and Carolina fell on the feast as ravenously as he did. She found a small rug to use as a tablecloth, right next to the windows so they could watch the wildlife while they lunched. The fare was simple, cinnamon bread for sandwiches, heaped with lettuce and cheese and shaved ham, almost too big to fit her mouth around. Pickles. Potato chips. Apple wedges. Plain old iced tea. Almond cookies.

No lobster here. No gilded spires or castle walls. He hoped she'd feel more down to earth in a more down-to-earth environment.

Maybe he'd been hoping it would work for him, too. For Pete's sake, she was wearing thick socks and baggy jeans and had cookie crumbs on her sweatshirt. How come he couldn't take his eyes off her? Her hair looked brushed by a cyclone, and she kept saying, "Look! Look!" when a woodpecker came to stare at them from the door sill…or when a squirrel checked them out from upside down on a tree limb.

A red-tailed hawk, four trees over, surveyed the vista below.

"If he goes swooping down on some prey, I'm not going to be happy," Carolina said darkly.

"Let me see."

"No. You've been hogging the binoculars since we got here. Oh, my God. Oh, my God. A mama deer, Maguire. With two half-grown fawns. Just lollygagging."

He grabbed the binocs, since she was being so stingy—and then she had to laugh. At him.

"I hate to tell you this," she teased, "but I'm not sure whether we're living my fantasy or yours."

"All right. I admit it. I just never thought of a tree house before, much less considered building one or spending time in one. It's terrific."

"Well, yeah. But you're the one who grew up in the lap of luxury. How come you never did this, if it was something fun for you? You made me make out that list. But have you ever done it? Made a list of things you really want to do?"

There now. She broke the spell. He forgot how annoying she could be—poking into corners he never poked into. He'd been content with his life before he met her. And she kept diverting him from the crisis problem—which was teaching her to be tough.

"We have more serious things we should talk over," he said abruptly. "We've talked about some general ideas, general plans and strategies you can try. But we've only skirted the really touchy stuff. For instance, you have a sister."

For one long instant, she looked at him. There was something in her eyes—besides sunbeams—but she seemed to decide to go along with the conversational tack he'd started. "Actually, I have a brother and a sister," she said.

"But it's the sister who leaned really hard on you, wasn't it? She started by asking you for a college education for her kids—"

"I wanted to do that!"

"Okay. I get that. But I'm not interested in what she asked you for. I want to hear, from you, what else you might want to do for your sister and your sister's family."

She started scooping up the debris from their lunch, stashing paper and napkins in a makeshift box. "I'd like her to have a nest egg. Just in case something traumatic happens. She's never said anything, but I know she doesn't have a great marriage. I think my brother-in-law's a cheater. Anyway. I was thinking about setting up a trust for her and her two kids. Not to just give them money outright. But so she'd know that she always had a door open, a way out, a kitty in the closet. I'd tell her about it. Tell her how I'm doing it, so she knows she's got this nest egg…but that it's not going to the Home Shopping Channel or to pay for something that would just disappear."

"She's not going to like that."

"I figure she won't either. She'll think I'm patronizing her. Or something like that." Carolina sighed. "But you asked what I wanted to do for her. And that's the deal."

"Hey."

"Hey what?"

"You're getting damn smart, Carolina."

"Of course I am. I've had a fabulous teacher. Holy

kamoly. Maguire! There's another hawk! Wait, wait. I think it's an eagle…"

Out of nowhere came a sudden civilized sound. His cell phone.

He froze, worried that he'd forgotten to tell Carolina that he'd needed to keep his cell on…worried that the sound of it would produce a panic response in her the way it had before.

Not this time. She heard it, looked at him, and he could almost see her shoulder muscles ease. It was just a phone. Not a threat. Phone calls weren't likely to threaten her ever again.

"I need to take this—" he started to say, but she just shook her head.

"Of course you do. No problem." And she whipped away the binoculars and turned back to the window, while he dug in his pocket for the cell.

It was his brother Jay, and he'd known Jay would call quickly after the last visit with Shannon. Maguire had fixed her problem—not just money, but removing her from the role of go-between. Once Jay discovered he would have to deal with someone who wasn't a vulnerable woman—namely himself—his brother was guaranteed to pursue communication. Jay had his penitent voice on, his excuses ready to spill.

"I was just in a little spot of trouble," Jay started in. "It was just cash flow."

"You know how many times you tried to sell me

this story?" Maguire moved as far away from Carolina as he could, kept his voice low.

"This time is different," his brother insisted.

"How?"

"I found a rehab place."

"And you've played that card before, too, Jay. You never meant it."

"This time I do. I'm going to end up with nothing and no one if I don't find a way to straighten up my act. This time I realize that."

"You've used those same words before. What I don't get is why you'd steal from your own brother. You don't even see Tommy. Don't give a damn how he's doing. Yet you'll do an end run with Shannon when you have more money than you could possibly want—"

"It was just a cash-flow thing. It won't ever happen again, I swear."

Maguire quit talking. He closed his eyes. Tried to listen. The call lasted several more minutes, and then Maguire clicked it off, then shut down the phone altogether. He faced the north glass wall without seeing anything, just standing there.

Behind him, he heard the door to the bathroom open. Then running water for a moment. Then silence again. His voice had been quiet; he knew it had been, and Carolina had obviously picked up that it was a private matter, steered out of the way. Maybe she hadn't heard. If she had, maybe his side of the conversation wouldn't make sense to her. No matter, if she just gave him a few more moments to get his head back on straight, he'd handle it fine.

But less than a millimoment passed before he felt a gentle hand on his shoulder.

He didn't want her sympathy or empathy. Not when he felt lower than dirt.

When he couldn't shake off her hand, she scooched around in front of him, leaning against the glass wall, taking the place of his view.

"Is that what you've been feeling bad about for the last couple days?" she asked gently.

"When the subject is my older brother, I've tended to feel bad from the day I was born. He has my father's fine, sterling character. No amount of money is ever enough. He always has a way of justifying whatever he does." He tried to make his tone sound light, as if the subject of his brother were at least halfway funny. Instead, he heard his voice come out terse and snappy. "Forget it, Carolina. The call's over with. It's not your problem. Just wasn't a pleasant thing to handle."

She nodded, as if she had the grace and courtesy and kindness to back away from something he obviously didn't want to talk about. Only, then she pounced again. Cocked her head, kept looking at his face, kept crowding him. With all that damn softness.

"You know, Maguire, you were the one who taught me about drawing lines in the sand. About how you have to draw clear lines to deal with some people. Lines, about what you're willing to do, what you're willing to give, how much you're willing to bleed for someone else. So…"

"So what?"

"So I have to believe you drew some extra-clear lines with your brother."

Damn, but she was annoying. "I sure as hell did. The line I drew in the sand with Jay is that I would never, ever sucker into him again. I'm through enabling him. He may be my brother, but he needs to accept real consequences for his behavior, and my helping him doesn't get that done."

She nodded again, still looking at him with all that empathy, even though he'd practically snapped her head off. Every word came out a snarl. Hell, his whole mind was a snarl.

"It sounds like you drew really good lines. Lines that put up clear boundaries that kept your brother from yanking your chain. Just like you've been trying to teach me to do with people who want to use me. Only…it sounds as if something happened when you talked to your brother and you caved."

"Exactly." Maguire didn't slug a fist into the glass wall for obvious reasons. But he wanted to. "I know better than to cave. Jay always plays the same card.

He knows the exact card that always works on me. Damn it. I want him to change. I want him to *want* a real life. I want him to have a relationship with Tommy. I want him to give a damn about something besides himself, for his own sake."

"So he promises you that…"

"And whenever he promises me that, I sucker in, like the stupidest fool ever born."

She cocked her head again. She had this way of looking like an innocent waif when she did that, not like a woman who was about to deliver a stinging zinger. "You know what?" she said softly. "Maybe it's okay if sometimes we can't hold tight to those lines. Maybe it's okay if sometimes the lines get blurry."

"No, it's *not* okay."

"Maybe this time will be the charm and your brother will actually mean what he promises."

"Oh, yeah. That'll be true when hell freezes over."

You'd think his tone of voice would have warned her off pursuing this topic. Instead, she seemed determined to wave a red flag in front of a bull. "Maguire…you feel responsible for so many people. You really work up a sweat about doing the right thing. I just think life is always touchier when it's about family. Next time, maybe you'll be able to say no. But even if you don't…I don't think it'd be all that awful if you cut yourself a little slack."

"What is this, the mentor suddenly turning into the mentee?"

"No, you big lummox," she said patiently. "It's about trying to crack open that hard, hard head of yours and letting someone else in."

"Like you, I suppose."

"Yup. Just like me. C'mere, Maguire. You're hurting. What's so terrible about letting someone else comfort you?"

She'd called him a lummox.

No one called him a lummox.

No one in the universe would think he was the kind of man who needed "comforting." The idea was idiotic. Absurd to the nth degree. So ridiculous, he couldn't believe it.

Touching her wasn't on his mind. Kissing her wasn't remotely on his agenda. He was just…aggravated…that was all. That she'd think he needed someone. That anyone as jaded and tough as himself would ever, ever lean on the Softie of the Universe. A man would never do that. Not a good man. A good man never preyed on the vulnerable.

And my God. She was softer than silver. Than pearls. Than a kitten's cry.

He didn't slam her up against the glass wall because he would never use aggression with a woman.

He didn't slam his mouth over hers, either. Same

reason. You didn't bruise roses. You never got rough with a lady.

He was just a tiny bit out of control. For that one small second.

And then she messed with his head. The way she'd been messing with his head from the second he met her.

She kissed him back, all hot and rough. She spread her hands up on that glass wall, inviting him to pin her harder, sharper. Inviting his chest to iron those soft, small breasts. For his pelvis to grind against her hips like some kind of dominant jungle idiot.

Maguire valued finesse.

He just couldn't find it for another minute. And while he was looking, searching, trying to figure out what had happened to him, how to apologize, how to backtrack…

Carolina flicked a wet tongue on his lips. Shivered her hips to nestle tight against him. Made sounds. Not soft sounds. Hissy sounds. Dares. Taunts.

Invitations.

Somehow she wriggled around, threw him off balance, and suddenly she had him against the glass wall, with the hundred-foot drop below…and a thousand-foot potential drop, from the expression in her eyes. She leaned him against that glass pane, risking life and limb. Sneaked her hands between their bodies to find the buttonhole of his jeans, the zipper.

Talk about a way to put combustible fuel in his engine.

"Wait," he said.

But she didn't. And he didn't, either. The truth was…hell, he didn't know what the truth was. Her taste, her scent, pushed every trigger he had. Her top peeled up; her jeans peeled down.

Where was the foreplay? Darned woman never did anything he could expect. You didn't start out with the zipper. You started out with tenderness. Any man knew that. But now there were all these windows, all that sunlight, all that nakedness.

He couldn't remember feeling this naked, this raw. Physically, yeah, of course. But not soul naked. Not with anyone.

She was just *there*. For him. The way no one had ever been there for him.

So maybe he couldn't put the cork back in the champagne. But she couldn't have everything her own way.

He lifted her, kissing her at the same time. Her legs swung tight around his waist and her eyes closed. He bumped a shin against something, cracked a toe on something else. Eventually he located the double beanbag chair, which was completely useless as a mattress.

It had potential, though.

He curled her on top of him, started on a long, lazy

tongue bath. He found a cookie crumb on her right breast, went searching for more. She convulsed in giggles when his tongue did the *Mission Impossible* thing—possibly not the response he was seeking—but damned if that laughter of hers didn't challenge him to make her laugh again.

He tried toe kisses. Behind-the-knee kisses. Upside-down kisses. Sideways kisses.

He tried strokes and rubs. He tried soft caresses, whispered touches…and then demanding pressure, bold kneading. He tried loving her with his eyes. He tried test after test, to discover what she liked, what moved her, what surprised her, what pleased her.

He loved her skin. Her lips. Her hair, the fine-lined scar on her shoulder, her bony knees, her sleek, slim body, the smell of her. And for a while, he was concentrating so hard, so fiercely, that he almost didn't realize that he was going out of his mind.

She was doing the same thing. Exploring him. Every which way. Her gaze intent, absorbed, her touch wild, then measured and tender. She shivered from thrill, then from…something else. And when she met his eyes, he thought maybe time had stopped forever.

He swished her beneath him, whispered, "Hold on, Cee."

She whispered, "You'd better hold on too, Maguire, because I'm not gonna be gentle."

How could there be laughter again, in the midst of so much tense tight need? Desire made his heart slam, his pulse skid, his body heat beyond boiling. Yet he flowed inside her, butter on butter, a smooth, tight, hot joining that made her cry out.

And urge him on.

A tumultuous ride of pure sensation, wild and free, sunlight flooding on her slim white body, her face, as if she were just that. Sunlight. Pure sunlight. The light in her seemed to reach him like nothing else ever had.

Her body suddenly arched, pleasure bursting from her in a cascade of shudders, and that light of hers, that heart-light, pushed him over the edge.

Later, she slept on his chest. He grabbed a jacket to cover her, but he didn't nap. He couldn't. Heaven knew what had just happened, but positively, it had never happened to him before. *She* had never happened to him before.

He was in love with her.

Forbidden or not, that's what it was. Right or wrong, there was no other name for it.

It was the craziest thing—at his advanced age of thirty-five, with all the complicated crazy life he'd already been through—to discover that he'd never been in love before.

He'd dealt with crisis his entire life. But never one this momentous or petrifying.

Chapter Ten

"Oh, my…oh, my…oh, my." Maybe she'd day-dreamed about spending the night in a tree house, but the reality was infinitely more wonderful. Right outside the window, on a nearby branch, perched an owl. A big owl. A big, beautiful whiteish owl. Just sitting there, where she and Maguire could look at him. "Isn't he magnificent?"

"Compared to you, no. Compared to other crea-tures—yeah, he's pretty damn amazing."

She twisted in his arms. The cushions on the floor made a mattress. Moonlight pouring in was brighter than any artificial light. She was scooped in his arms, using one of his arms as a pillow, his other arm tucked around her, both of them naked beneath a mound of sleeping bags. "Did you just call me magnificent, Maguire?"

"Couldn't have."

"Because it sounded like it."

"You misheard. Or it was a slip of the tongue, because it's so late and we're both tired."

"We're both tired because *you* were so magnificent."

Oops. Wrong thing to say. He tensed up like a shutter slamming out sunlight. For a while, he'd been lazy and relaxed, the Maguire she knew could be coaxed out of hiding. He was a man who laughed, teased her, took teasing back, inhaled the silver-and-black-velvet night out there with the same relish she did.

Apparently he forgot he was the relentless alpha-male Maguire for a few hours…but now he went quiet on her again. It occurred to her—it kept occurring to her—that she'd used silence as a way to protect herself in a very similar way. Maguire might not have a case of hysterical deafness, but just like her, he'd found a way to shut himself off from things that were threatening to him.

"Hey, lover," she murmured, trying to capture his attention, and of course, she did. She got "the eyebrow" at the use of the endearment. "The tree house is impossibly wonderful. I'm really glad you found it."

"Me, too. I can't believe I never even thought about one before."

"It's such a perfect hideaway. Nothing big to take care of. Just a place to hide out. Forget civilization for a while." Without skipping a beat, she segued into the topic on her mind and heart. "Maguire, if you're feeling guilty because of something to do with me—don't."

His head swiveled toward hers immediately. His eyes looked huge and dark in the moonlight. "Want some wine?"

"Nope. Just want to say…I'm hugely glad we did this."

"Good," he snapped.

She'd survived putting her finger in an electric socket before. And was willing to risk it again. For him. "You know," she murmured, "I have every right to love you if I want to. Every right to admit that you turn me way, way on. To admit that I care for you. To admit that I've never felt…this kind of desire before. And that I'm old enough to throw caution to the winds and do something just for myself." When he didn't respond—how easy for Maguire to shut up and dodge her that way—she said bluntly, "You care a lot for me too."

"Of course I do."

"No. Not like a big brother. Not like a responsibility. I mean…the lover kind of caring."

"Do we really have to have this talk?"

"Uh-huh." She nodded vigorously, propped up on an elbow.

He sighed, heavier than a north winter wind. "Here's the thing. This shouldn't have happened. The making love. The problem is…your vulnerability. I came into your life to right a wrong, to fix things. Making love with you was taking advantage."

"Hello. Do you remember my participation both times? Did you have to sell me tickets?"

"Two weeks ago you were crushed."

"Yeah, I was. A mess. But that was then. I wanted this. You wanted this. We're both bringing trust and respect and a whole lot of plain chemistry to the table. I don't see anyone getting hurt in this scenario."

"You could be hurt."

"Maybe. But isn't that what you said our time together was about? Making me tougher. Making me stand up for what I want and need. Making *me* decide what's right for me and how to go about it."

"Carolina. You're not in love with me. This is just a moment in time. Two weeks. Not a vacation from life, but a moratorium on stress. Nothing you want or do is wrong. I just don't want you getting long-term hopes—or fears—that are distracting. I want you going back to your life feeling strong and good."

She leaned closer. Touched his bottom lip with

her fingertip, saw his eyes, that flash-fast spark with fire.

"Okay," she said, "but what I've been trying to tell you, Maguire, is that you're exactly what I needed. Not just the mentoring lessons and all the spoiling. But you, specifically you. Making love with me. There's no guilt or wrong. What you've been with me has helped me become stronger."

"That sounds real good, Ms. Toughie. But it doesn't make sense."

"You're not a woman. It makes perfect sense to me." She touched his arm—not in invitation, not about the discussion, but to motion him outside. The white owl had spotted prey somewhere in the darkness. One instant he was perched high and silent, the next soaring, swooping down…silent and beautiful.

"I have the feeling a mouse is going to have a very bad night," Maguire murmured.

"But our owl has to eat too. He's been sitting there for hours in the cold." Like Maguire, she thought. He took it for granted. That he'd always be alone in the cold. "Okay, you."

"Okay, what?"

"Okay, I know you're sick of talking. That you don't like this kind of talk. So I just want to say one more thing and then you're free."

"No. Nothing good ever follows after a woman says she only wants to say one more thing."

She grinned. But not for long. She went soft and quiet. "You made me reexamine my life, Maguire. Made me think about all the things I've yearned for or wanted—and most of them, I figured out, aren't about money at all. They're about fun. And wonder. And new experiences. And wanting richness—not money richness, but richness in life experiences and relationships with people."

"Yeah. That was exactly where I was hoping you'd go. Not letting anyone define stuff for you. Defining what you want and need for itself."

"And I get it. You've been a fabulous mentor."

"Good."

"But what about *you?*" she whispered. "How come you're alone? You've never wanted a wife, kids, that kind of personal life? What do you do in your free time that makes you happy?"

He shot her a familiar look of impatience, even as he stroked the curve of her shoulder. "When you're ten years old, you worry about what'll make you happy. When you're an adult, I'm not so sure that "happy" is a meaningful criterion of anything."

"Okay. We'll use a different word. You, being you, need to feel productive at the end of a day."

He glanced at her. "Yeah, I do. If I haven't accomplished concrete things at the end of a day, I feel off kilter."

She nodded. "You have to make a difference. You

have to behave by your own high standards—whether anyone else is looking or not. You have to live by what you believe in, no matter what anyone else says or thinks."

He rolled his eyes, as if that evaluation were true of everyone. "Okay, so where are you going with all this?"

"Here's the point. Have you ever done what you asked me to do? Make a list. A list of things you'd like to do or see. Then go after those things. Name them. Protect them. Get them on your life agenda."

"I've got what I need," he said impatiently.

Yeah, she thought. And *she* wasn't on the list.

How could she expect otherwise? They'd known each other for the briefest of times, under only extraordinary circumstances. Their backgrounds were different, their families, education, everything. When it came down to it, they had nothing in common except for Tommy.

And that she'd fallen hopelessly, helplessly in love with him.

"Okay, you," she said. "No more talking. You have what you need. I got it. But…"

"More talking?"

"Nope," she whispered. "I was just going to show you one eensy-teensy thing that you might still need tonight."

"No. Not that. Anything but that."

"Shut up and take being seduced like a man, Maguire," she said gruffly, and then, gently, "although, you can offer a suggestion here and there if you feel like it. I'm a believer in making rolling readjustments."

"Are you now?"

Her man was thirsty and hungry. Not for water or food. For sustenance of the heart. But…

She was about to give him a second helping. Something to hold him for a while.

Because she was leaving after that. She knew it. He knew it.

And she had absolutely no way to stop it.

A day had never passed so fast. Maguire never specifically said, "That's it, back to real life now"— and neither did she. Carolina didn't need to talk about an elephant in the living room to know it was there.

Chores followed chores—the MG had been returned, the messes from their overnight in the tree house dismantled and taken back to the lodge, then the lodge tackled. She put her belongings together, cleaned the fridge. Maguire made heaps of phone calls and worked to make the lodge "turn key," prepared for an absence.

At some point, the schedule went on the table. At ten in the morning, Henry would fly her directly to South Bend, and see that she was settled back at her place. Maguire had a temporary business thing in Denver, after which he was disappearing back to wherever else he lived, whatever else he did.

There was only one way she could handle this, Carolina determined, and she bounced down the stairs a few minutes before ten the next morning. She was wearing her red shoes, old jeans, new sunglasses, her hair all flyaway and her cheerfulness out front, brassy and brazen.

With only minutes left, she wanted him to see exactly what she wasn't. A princess. A well-mannered, well-bred, perfect type of rich man's wife. She was what she was—a teacher who came from a blue-collar background. Who was going to love her red shoes until the day she died. Who loved sleeping with owls. And pigging out on lobster. And who was always going to have to work at certain flaws in her character, because they were pretty close to unchangeable.

"Okay, let's get these goodbyes over with and this show on the road. Kiss," she demanded of Henry. Who pecked her properly, even as he stood in the door with her luggage.

She pranced over to Maguire, her cheerfulness beaming even brighter. "Kiss," she demanded.

He held her by the shoulders, his grip just a little too tight, his eyes just a little too dark. "Listen," he said.

"No. I've listened to you until I'm blue in the face. You've taught me all you're going to teach me, big guy. But I've got advice for you. Don't kidnap any other women, okay?"

He grinned, but the smile faded away, and still he held on to her shoulders. "When you were a kid, I'll bet you read a book by Shel Silverstein. *The Giving Tree.*"

She blinked in surprise. "Well, yeah, who hasn't? I adored it."

"That's what you need to guard for, Carolina. Your nature is to be that giving tree. But you can't do that—give and give and give—without stripping yourself bare. You put up your boundaries. You get tough."

"Yes, sir. Are you going to give Tommy a big hug from me?"

"Yes."

"Are you going to let me visit him sometime? And vice versa?"

"Absolutely yes."

"So where's my kiss goodbye, Maguire?"

She was trying to sound saucy and sassy and fun. But he didn't want to kiss her. She could see it. She could feel it, like a knife twisting in her heart, a sharp ache of awareness. He might want her. He might like being with her. He might even love her, to a point.

But he didn't want to.

She was just a project for him. A responsibility. A problem he had to fix.

"Okay, okay," she said teasingly. "No kiss for you. Just know, I'm not about to forget you."

She made it inside the plane before she started crying. Henry didn't see her, nor did the copilot up front. Both were locked in the front cabin, while she had the whole fancy back to herself. A down blanket and poofy pillows were set up for her to nap, a gourmet lunch with cold shrimp and lobster dripping ice whenever she wanted it.

All she wanted was to find some Kleenex.

The trip was around four hours, and by the time the jet landed, her eyes were over-dry, but she'd tidied up everything in back—washed her few dishes, folded up the blanket, nothing out of place, as if she'd never been there. Henry came through from the front and took one narrow-eyed look at her face.

"Are we doing okay?" he asked tactfully.

"Of course we are."

"Mr. Cochran set up a car waiting."

"Of course he did," she said hollowly.

Henry drove her from the airport to her old apartment. Carolina thought the short drive was a little like landing on Mars. All the familiar landmarks seemed to be someone else's landmarks. She knew the roads, the restaurants, the gold dome of Notre Dame, the infamous Grape Road—but none of them gave her a feeling of being home.

Her apartment was the worst, although Henry kept

up a steady patter to fill her in. "We had your car checked out, tires, gas, oil, all that, because we didn't know what shape it was in when you left."

"Thanks, Henry."

"It was Mr. Cochran who did it all, really. I wouldn't have thought of all the specifics and details, not the way he did. In the meantime, your regular e-mail and phones have been turned back on. I've got a folder of contacts—who we contacted, so they'd know you were all right. And who was trying to reach you. You realize we'd have given you the communications before if there'd been any kind of emergency—"

"Of course," she said.

"Like a family illness or anything like that. Mr. Cochran was only trying to give you a break from demands on you for that short stretch."

"Of course," she said.

"I took the liberty of having your fridge stocked with just a few things. Fresh milk, fresh eggs. Bread. Not much. But so you wouldn't have to immediately run to the store." He hefted the two suitcases from the trunk—she'd gone with nothing; and come home with cases that were chock-full. "I'll return your key. And I have a list of phone numbers here. Mr. Cochran. Myself. The list of contacts he discussed with you before. So if you need anything—anything at all—"

"Henry, Maguire fixed me. Completely. I won't need anything from anyone. I promise."

Finally, he set down the suitcases, then stood at the front door like an awkward geek who didn't know how to stay or go. She said, "If you stand there a minute more, I'll throw my arms around your neck to thank you for all you've done for me."

That did it. He took an immediate step back, eyes wide with alarm, and reached for the door. He said, "I think you're the best thing that ever happened to him, Carolina." And then left, hiking back to the rental car at a speed designed to outwit robbers, bill collectors…or women who might hug him without restraint.

Then she was alone, for the first time in quite a while.

She wandered through the four rooms, feeling like a cat trying to find the right spot to settle. The apartment had been cleaned stem to stern. The sinks shined. The pink towels in the bathroom were hung straight. The book she'd been reading was still face-down on her nightstand—but dusted—and her gold-leaf lamp, a treasure inherited from her grandmother, gleamed when she flicked on the light.

She'd decorated every inch of the place—some from Ikea, some from yard sales, some from family attics, pulling together colors and textures she liked. When everyone first heard about the inheritance, they'd all urged her to move to a nicer place.

She could. But the reason the apartment no longer

felt like home had nothing do with furnishings or style or any other details like that. It was about feeling the absence of Maguire.

She would have to get used to it, she told herself. As crazy as it sounded, he was where her home was. Her heart. But that, of course, was foolish thinking.

A sudden sound jarred her thoughts—the phone. Her phone, her landline.

Two weeks ago, she'd caved at that torturous sound. Now she gulped and strode toward the phone. She'd left a life dangling.

She wasn't ducking and running from anything that mattered to her, ever again.

Maguire was on a video cam when Henry yelled out a hello. Henry'd been gone for three days. Maguire had been chasing his own heels the whole time, working nonstop. The video cam was essentially a business call between an Austrian, Japanese and British counterpart—it was no mean feat to find a time and time zone where they could all comfortably talk together. Their common project was still in the engineering stage, but they'd all invested several million. It was time to separate the men from the boys, so to speak. The lady from Austria very definitely was tough, but the discussion was tricky and complicated. Everybody might have their feet in the same water, but they each had sharply different ideas about how to swim to the other side.

Henry showed up in the office doorway, saw what was happening, waved a greeting and disappeared—undoubtedly to raid the kitchen, Maguire assumed.

He couldn't cut the video meeting short. It had taken hell times ten to put it together to begin with. The project mattered. It was one of his babies right now, in spite of the precarious economy.

But he was as distracted as a porcupine with an itch. He finally got all the business accomplished and severed the call. Two in the morning was a tough time to negotiate. He jogged toward the living room, hoping to hell Henry wasn't already asleep.

He wasn't. Looking, as always, impeccable in unwrinkled sweater and slacks, he had the television on in the kitchen, some war flick, a tidy sandwich in one hand and a beer stein in the other.

"All hell's broken loose since you were gone," Maguire said, and started the fill him in. Henry was due some R&R. Maguire had fires burning in Atlanta, Chicago, a sort-out with Jay in the middle, a stupid speech he'd somehow signed up for in D.C. Wednesday night. He was behind, of course, from having disappeared for the last two weeks.

"I need you home—"

"Which home, sir?"

"I'm going to base out of the Chicago condo for

the next while. I need you to call, get things opened up, food, all that—"

"Yes, sir."

"Would you mind contacting Billingham for me. He'll be expecting a call, and I know I won't get to it. Folder's on the desk—"

"Yes, sir."

"If he still has a question, contact me."

"Yes, sir."

"Did we get a new security set up for the Elkon system?" Maguire poked around in the fridge, saw beer, milk, finally pushed aside debris, found some fresh OJ.

"No. You put that on hold until next month."

"Well, let's push it up again. It's been on my mind. There's too much to protect to let that slide. Scare up the bids again, would you?"

"Yes, sir."

"Now, on Carolina. Let the weekend go, but check on her Monday."

"No, sir."

Maguire closed the fridge, turned around. "Beg your pardon?"

"I said no, sir. I'm not spying on Carolina."

Maguire frowned. A headache had been playing slice-and-dice in his temples for three days. He was used to pressure. Used to having an impossibly heavy schedule. Used to finding discipline and endurance when there couldn't be any left.

He just wasn't used to pain having this fist-grip on his heart.

"I wasn't asking you to *spy* on her, Henry. I was asking you to check in."

Mild as milquetoast, Henry said again, "No." And turned off the tube.

"You work for me, remember? I give the instructions. You say yes, and then follow through better than I would myself. That's your job. And you're great at it."

"Yes, sir. Although you can outwork anyone I ever met."

"Which is the point. I'm extremely busy. And it's not as if I were asking you to do anything. I just need to know that Carolina's all right."

Henry stood up from the couch, dusted two crumbs from his trousers, took the sandwich plate to the kitchen and neatly slid it in the dishwasher. "I understand your concern, Mr. Cochran. That Carolina, she just isn't of the me-me-me generation. I don't doubt she can look after herself. I just think she could easily fall into her old ways."

Maguire picked up that beat as if it had been on his mind. "Giving in to everybody. Riding herself ragged for everyone else. The calls will have restarted by now. Her family and friends and all will realize she's back home. It'll start up again. I think she's stronger. I think she has good ideas on what to do. Stuff she *can* do. But I need to be sure."

"Then call her yourself, sir."

"I beg your pardon?"

Henry didn't seem to hear. He aimed for the stairs, as if intending to crash for the night. "I keep remembering how she was when you first brought her here. Not hearing. Jumping at every shadow. I just think it'd be easy for her to get over her head again. I'm not all that positive you can teach a kitten to be tough."

"Which is precisely why I want you to follow up and make sure she's all right."

"Well, I would, Mr. Cochran, because I'm not looking to get fired. I love my job. I can't even imagine a job as good as this one. But she's not my business, sir. She's yours. If you don't mind my saying, I almost didn't recognize you when I walked in here. You obviously haven't slept or showered or apparently eaten since I left. You look like hell, sir, and that's putting it as politely as I can. I fully recognize that you've never appreciated advice—"

"Then it would probably be extremely wise for you to shut the *h* up, Henry."

"But in my opinion, you don't just need to call her. You need to find her. I have no idea what was wrong with the men in South Bend in the past, but they can't all be shallow and blind. Someone is going to take a look and have the sense to realize that she's absolutely one of a kind."

Maguire's eyes narrowed. "You think I don't know that? But she's not a keeper for *me,* Henry. I kidnapped her, remember? She didn't ask me to be in her life."

"So if she needs help now, you wouldn't be there?"

"Don't be ridiculous. I'd be there in two seconds."

"Then call her yourself. To find out if she's all right or not." Henry's voice rose a full decibel before he shut down and turned around, stiff-necked and red-cheeked. "I'm going to bed, sir."

Maguire didn't answer, just stared after Henry. He'd never heard Henry yell before. Henry didn't even raise his voice for football games or tornados.

He could have fired him, of course, but Maguire couldn't imagine doing that for a single indiscretion. It wasn't as if Henry regularly—or ever—stepped out of line, or had given Maguire any reason to doubt his dedication.

Henry was loyal. Apparently he'd picked up some mighty loyalty to Carolina as well.

Henry just didn't understand, Maguire thought glumly. Once he'd kidnapped Carolina, everything changed. He'd had good reasons to steal her off, but the "force" word was the bear. She'd been *forced* to be with him.

Now…it would have been easy, so easy to call her, fly to see her, tell her he'd fallen crazy in love with her, that nothing had been right since she left. It was the truth.

But it was also the truth that he couldn't, ethically or morally, force Carolina to be with him again on any terms. To manipulate another situation would be the act of a control freak, not a lover. A bully, not a man hopelessly in love.

How could he ever know how she really felt if she'd never been free to make her own choices?

So he'd tied his own hands.

And it was killing him.

Chapter Eleven

Carolina parked in front of the old, redbrick house with a feeling of doom and gloom. Naturally, the wind was blowing up a tempest, shaking all the red-and-gold leaves, slapping her cheeks, sneaking down the neck of her old plaid jacket. She loved her parents, she reminded herself.

She was just looking forward to this particular visit on a par with, say, a double root canal.

She pulled a satchel, packages and bottle of wine from the backseat, then had to juggle them as she walked up the familiar brick path to the back door. "Mom! Dad!" she called out.

She'd spent a couple days feeling sorry for herself…

and trying to face that she'd never likely see Maguire again. The woman he'd kidnapped wasn't the kind of woman who belonged in his life. Things might have been different if they could have met like normal people. But they hadn't.

It just didn't pay to be kidnapped.

Rather than pine and whine any longer, she figured she'd better face her demons.

Her mom showed up in the doorway first, her dad stepping on her heels. Her mother was wearing a tiger print, had new highlights in her chin-length bob, wore snazzy red-framed glasses—and hurled herself at Carolina with a sob, a hug and a fog of Chanel No 19.

"Honey, I've missed you so much! I don't understand why you went off like that! Why you'd ever shut us out! I was so worried and upset! I just don't understand!"

Then her dad took over, enveloped her in a giant hug with tears in his eyes. "I'm so glad you're home again, princess. Your mom was terribly upset. Not me. I know you're a big girl, and can take of yourself. We're just used to being able to talk to you whenever we want to."

"I know. And I'm so sorry, both of you." Actually, Carolina knew they'd been told where she was, and how to contact her in case of an emergency. Her parents just couldn't conceive of any occasion where they couldn't immediately reach her. She wasn't about to get into Maguire and the kidnapping, but they needed some explanations.

And she needed to face them as well.

Wine got poured. The wailing went on for a while. Apple pie slowed it down. So did the presents she'd brought for both of them. Eventually they all sat in the rust-and-brown den—no one ever sat in her mother's living room; life revolved around the TV. Family pictures dominated the walls, her mom's angel collection dominated the bookshelves and her father's latest model took up half the coffee table. All of it was as familiar as her childhood, evoked equal amounts of love and stress.

As did the conversation.

Her father hunched forward at a gesture from her mom, making Carolina guess that they'd choreographed this talk ahead of time. "Honey, your mother and I have been thinking. We think it's a good idea for us to move in with you. Or, if you'd rather, that you move in with us."

"Dad, that's not necessary," she said quickly.

"We think it is. We understand that you're grown up, that the last thing a young single woman would normally want is parents looking over her shoulder. But this whole inheritance business has been too much for you."

"We can protect you," her mother chimed in. "Take

care of things. Your dad could handle the finances, and I could take charge of your place, redecorating or whatever you need. We'll take the stress off…"

Before this got any hairier, Carolina stood up, opened the satchel she'd brought in. "You two are both right. I wasn't handling stress well. But actually, one thing I needed to figure out had nothing to do with me. It was about you two. And, Dad, I need to ask you a favor."

"Anything, princess."

Carolina pulled out the sheaf of papers. "This is the paperwork for a trust that I created for you and Mom. It's set up to give you two a monthly discretionary allowance, but there's a lot of give-and-take in the setup. You might want something bigger now and then—like a car or a trip or something? Then you'd have to figure out how to work that out with taxes and social security and all."

Before her parents could say anything, Carolina said quickly, "It's just all too much for me. I needed some expert advice. That's partly what I've been doing for the past two weeks. Getting that advice. Getting a crash course in finances from experts. That wasn't hard. But it would be hard for me to handle this trust on top of everything else, so I was hoping that between you and Mom—"

"Carolina," her mother said firmly, "I still feel you

need us close by. This whole new lifestyle has put so much pressure on you, and—"

"Ruth Marie." Her dad had been looking over the papers, had homed in on some of the bottom-line numbers.

"Don't interrupt me," her mother started to say, but her dad sank back on the couch and grabbed her mother's hand to make her sit down with him.

"I'm stunned, honey," he said. "And of course I'll take this on. You're the most wonderful daughter…"

She wasn't sure Maguire would give her the same heaps of credit. She'd narrowly escaped having her parents live with her. Much as she loved them, it was that kind of suffocation that made her so crazy… weeks ago? Was it really only weeks ago?

It was dark when she left her parents' place, but she had one more thing to do before going home. The drive to Kalamazoo was a long two hours, but it was a city where she knew no one. It only took a few extra minutes to find an outside U.S. postal box.

She slipped the package in, and finally headed home.

"Sir."

Maguire woke at the sound of the phone, and glanced, bleary eyed, at the hotel bedside clock. Maybe it was only eleven at night, but he'd been running nonstop for almost a week, had been sleeping like the dead. Naturally he immediately recognized Henry's voice.

"Okay. Two immediate things, Mr. Cochran. Tommy insisted I call you and tell you that he won a prize for 'most improved in speech.'"

"Thank you, Henry. That'll take a reward, I'm thinking, when I get back."

"That's why I thought you'd want to know, sir. In case you wanted to contact him tomorrow."

"And?"

Henry reeled off a number of business issues, none of which really required a call, and then suddenly suffered a dry cough. "A package arrived for you. I opened it, sir."

"You're telling me this why?"

"Well, sir, I wouldn't have opened it if it had been marked Private. Obviously. I was just going through the regular—"

"Tell me what was in it, Henry, before I fall back asleep."

"A T-shirt, sir." Another discreet cough. "Gray. Light gray. A nice cotton. With a logo. It says, For the Sexually Gifted."

Maguire's eyes startled open. "What!"

"It's postmarked Kalamazoo, Michigan."

"I don't know anyone in Kalamazoo, Michigan."

"Well, Mr. Cochran, someone in Kalamazoo

seems to think quite highly of you. In that one re-gard. I mean, if they don't know you, they're cer-tainly making some interesting assumptions. And if the person does know you, then she seems to feel a unique motivation to applaud your, um—"

"That's enough, Henry. You're *sure* there's no note?"

"No note. No return address. Just the postmark."

"Quit laughing, Henry."

"I'm not laughing, sir. I just couldn't think of any-one in the universe who would have sent you this. I mean, no offense, sir. It's not the grade score I was thinking about. It was the humor of it. I don't know anyone in your circle of people who would have—"

Neither did Maguire. He had many, many acquain-tances and business friends and family connections and work and charity people he knew. Most, he had a cordial relationship. Some, more.

None, though, with that kind of irreverent sense of humor.

None. Not a single soul.

It didn't make sense.

When Carolina opened the door, her sister strode in, handed her a package, started talking and never stopped. "I don't know who delivered this thing, but you must not have heard them knocking. Isn't it crazy? And, Caro, why on earth are you still living in this dump?"

Carolina was momentarily stunned at the package—M&M's in a glass apothecary jar, labeled Tough Pills. She believed in miracles. Always had. But the only person who could conceivably find a way to leave that particular present on her doorstep—well, it was a stunner, that's all. It made her heart suddenly thump like a jackhammer.

Donna, in the meantime, was shedding leather jacket, shoes and scarf, still talking. "Come on, Carolina. You don't even have the security you need here. This place is ridiculous for someone with the money you have now."

"Actually...I intend to move. There just hasn't been time."

"That's so you. Your priorities are never like anyone else's. Some of us have a tougher road, you know. I'd rather be like you. Do what I want, when I want. I never planned to be a realist."

When Carolina had asked Donna for a visit, she'd expected trouble. "Things not going so well with Mike?"

"He lost his job. Again." Donna rooted in the fridge, emerged with a soda, popped the top. Her blond hair was shoulder length. She still had the cheerleader body, the great smile, the gorgeous skin. The red-piped sweater and jeans fit her perfectly.

Growing up, Carolina had always known Donna was the beauty in the family, but lines had settled in around her sister's eyes and mouth.

"You've been dealt your share," Carolina said sympathetically.

"I have. I swear to God. I look back now, and wonder how I could have ever believed Mike would hold a long-term job. I mean, he's the same guy I married. Lots of fun. Great with the kids. Always happy to play. Just doesn't have a single responsible bone in his entire body."

"The kids?" Carolina watched her sister throw herself on the couch with a major sigh. Apparently the kids weren't going to be an easy topic either.

"The kids are just like all the other teenagers today. Spoiled rotten. None of them appreciate how hard I've had to work, what I do for them. Mike gets to be the fun parent. I haven't been fun in a long time."

Carolina plunked down in the microfiber chair, still holding the apothecary jar. Slowly, she unsealed it, and popped in one of the tough pills. Her sister was still going on.

"Carolina…maybe this isn't the right thing to be honest about. But I resent your money. I resent that you suddenly got real estate on easy street without having to do anything for it. I just don't know how to act around you."

"What's wrong with being like we always were?"

"No. It's not the same. It'll never be the same again."

Carolina popped another tough pill. Then reconsidered and scooped up three, all red ones. "I've got the papers I told you about. The kids' education account. A nest-egg trust for you, with me as cosigner, that your husband has no access to. No matter what happens, you'll be okay."

"That's nice. That's a big thank-you. But what if I can't make payments on our house? What if Jimmy gets in trouble with the law again? What if my car breaks down?"

"You're strung tighter than wire, Donna."

"I know I'm being bitchy. I know. I'm just exhausted all the time. And you've got all this money, while I feel like a nothing and a no one. Mike says I should ask you for a house. Like, why should he have to work when he's got a rich sister-in-law?"

"And what did you tell him?" Carolina considered another tough pill, but decided the ones she'd had were working.

"That I wasn't asking you for a new house." But she was. It was in Donna's eyes, not greed, but the pain of envy. "Mike got really mad at me. He said you were selfish. All about yourself. While we're the ones with growing kids and job troubles."

Carolina doubted that Mike had actually said that. Donna was the only one in the family who'd ever called her selfish. Donna, who married the high school football star and always expected her life would be golden.

"Donna, you're not going to agree with me on this. But I don't see the inheritance as totally mine."

"Of course it is!"

"Legally," Carolina agreed. "But the exciting part for me is getting to do something. Having enough money to make a difference. Having the chance to do something that matters to me."

"Your family doesn't matter to you? I don't matter to you?"

"Yes. Of course the family matters. Of course you do. But no amount of money would make you happier with Mike, would it? Or make the kids any more appreciative?"

"Maybe it would. Maybe money would do all those things. For sure it would take away all the worry and heartache, let us live easier. I don't understand you, Caro. You're just thinking about what you want! What matters to you!"

When her sister left, Carolina threw herself on the couch and winced—even though there was no one there to see. She'd handled that on a par with an elephant in a china shop. Predictably, her sister had made her feel guilty and small and selfish. She'd wanted to cave in with every harsh word.

But she couldn't have Maguire believing that his tough pills hadn't worked.

She didn't want him believing that he'd made love to the Wimp of the Universe.

Maybe she hadn't suddenly turned into a brilliantly strong person. But she hadn't caved. She'd done what she thought was right and reasonable. And now, Carolina considered, she deserved a reward.

So she jumped to her feet, grabbed a coat and car keys, and hightailed it to a bookstore. She had just the thing in mind.

There was a spit of snow in the area when Maguire arrived back at the lodge. He'd worked himself crazy for the last two weeks, but now he had a break. It's not as if there was ever a complete shutoff button on responsibilities, but he planned some Tommy time, some walk-in-the-woods time—and some serious rest.

His eyes were stinging tired, his stomach restless. Henry barely spoke to him on the ride home—but then Henry had barely spoken a civil word to him since he'd let Carolina go.

It was pitch-black—except for the shards of ice coming from the sky—when they stumbled from the car with their gear. Maguire had the key out and ready, pushed open the door, flipped on a light.

Par for the course, Henry had left the current

mail on the table, where Maguire could go through it over coffee the next morning. He saw the pile, and wouldn't have hesitated to leave it, except for the box on top.

The postmark was Elkhart, Indiana. No one he knew or had ever known was from Elkhart. The box was square, bigger than a shoe box and heavy.

Behind him, Henry carted in bags, locked up, aimed for the fridge. Normally he'd have gone straight to bed, but he'd obviously seen Maguire pick up the package.

"Just came in yesterday," Henry said.

"It'll wait until morning."

"Sure will." But Henry didn't move because Maguire didn't. Damn, but he couldn't stand mysteries or undotted *i*'s. So he peeled off the wrapping. Three hefty books fell in his lap. *Plans to Build Your Own Tree House, How to Build Your Own Tree House,* and *Tree Houses—Hideouts for Grown-ups.*

Maguire felt something knot, tight and thick, in his throat, as he paged through them. There was no note. No signed anything. Eventually he glanced up to see Henry staring at him.

"That damn woman," Maguire said.

"That's what I was thinking, sir," Henry agreed.

"She doesn't play fair."

"She certainly doesn't."

"This isn't honest warfare. She's being sneaky,

even sneakier than me. It's just not right. It's under the table. It's a low way of getting to a man."

"I thought the same thing, Mr. Cochran. The minute I laid eyes on her, I thought, well, no one like her has ever been in Mr. Cochran's life. She doesn't play by his rules."

"She misled me, Henry. I thought she was a good woman. A decent woman. An honest woman. And then she does something like this. It's unconscionable." Maguire paced around, shot a finger at Henry, then paced some more. "This changes things. I've tried to do the right thing. I've *tried*. But damn it, if she refuses to play fair, why should I be the only one suffering?"

"Now you're talking, sir."

Carolina was just pulling a major chunk of mail from her mailbox when she saw her brother pull in to the driveway. She jogged over to give him an enormous hug. "Come on in, you sweetie! Want some coffee?"

Gregg had on his old high school jacket, and was wearing his hair a little long. He was the one who'd found her weeks ago, raised all the flags for help, got her to the hospital. Back when they were in high school, he'd started football, quit. Started college, quit. Started one job after another, quit. Gregg never heard of an idea involving quick money that he didn't fall for—but Carolina loved him, warts and all.

"You're looking good. For a sister." He ruffled her new haircut while she thumped down the mail and started a fresh pot of coffee. "Hey. I had an idea."

"Yeah?" She paged through the heap of mail, tossing out the junk mail, separating the bills…and then stopped. Her heart, her head, everything stopped.

She saw Maguire's Washington return address. Opened the heavy envelope, found a fat, thick catalog. It was for an auction in Paris, of last year's designer shoes. She paged through, her throat thickening. There were pages and pages and pages of frivolous, uselessly, miserably uncomfortable, gorgeous shoe designs.

My God. How dirty could Maguire get? How ugly? And by using his real return address, he'd of course identified himself as the culprit—upping the ante.

"It's just…" Gregg knew where her mugs were, poured two cups. "I've got an idea for a start-up business, sis. A coffee shop. I know, there's lots of those. But most of them are really expensive and fancy. What if I started a place that served really good coffee, but cheap. I've got a friend…"

Her head shot up, although her finger was still stroking the page with the ostrich sandals.

"He's got the coffee. He's got the plan. We just need some seed money to get it going—"

Temporarily, only temporarily, she closed the shoe catalog. "You know what, Gregg? One of the cold hard truths I've tried to face in the last month is that I'm just plain terrible with numbers."

"That's not a problem, sis. See—"

She carefully interrupted again. "So I decided I'd better not make financial decisions myself. I've researched some really good people, with terrific reputations. If you want to give them a business plan, I'll tell them you're my brother. But actual decisions on issues like this, I've moved out of my hands."

Gregg's jaw dropped. "But it's your money."

"I know. But I wouldn't do my own brain surgery. Or fill my own cavities. Same with this, you know. This isn't something I'm good at, so I found people who were."

"But I'm your brother."

"And I couldn't love you more in a million, thousand years."

Her brother left twenty minutes later, not too happy with her, but that was okay. Someday maybe family could have a conversation with her without asking for money—but if not, not.

She had more interesting things to worry about.

She jogged back to the catalog, thumbing through it again, page by page. That damn man. Tempting her with shoes. How low could a man get? What happened to Maguire's integrity, his honor?

And if he'd sink this low…just maybe she could entice him to sink a wee bit lower.

Like down to her level.

Chapter Twelve

"Sir! Mr. Cochran! Sir!"

Maguire and Tommy both turned at the same time. They'd only ambled a half mile into the woods when they suddenly heard Henry's voice. Maguire had never seen Henry run hell-bent for leather before.

Henry reached them, put his hands on his knees, heaving in breath. "Sir, you need to go back to the house."

"Are you all right? What's wrong?"

"It's not me. *I'm* fine. But at the house—" Henry motioned, still breathing too hard to talk well. "She's done something."

Henry could have been referring to any number of

"she's" worldwide, but there was probably only one that could induce that panic-stricken gallop across the woods. "Is Carolina ill? Hurt? Need help?" Maguire asked swiftly.

"Nothing like that. You and Tommy. Just go back to the house. You'll see."

Maguire had already started running back to the lodge, Tommy keeping pace beside him—but it was Tommy who surged ahead when they reached sight of the back door, Tommy who let out a squeal loud enough to wake the mountains.

The dog sitting on the porch step seemed to have a foot-long tongue—and a five-foot-long tail, which immediately started wagging when Tommy ran toward him. The golden retriever looked to be full grown, extra big, extra golden. Maguire shouted a warning to Tommy, who paid no attention, just surged toward the unfamiliar dog with his arms outstretched.

Tommy had no sense of caution. He knocked the dog over, and himself at the same time. Maguire reached them both in seconds, but not fast enough to prevent Tommy from giggling to high heavens as the retriever lavishly, lovingly washed his face.

Henry brought up the rear, still panting like a racehorse. "There was a note attached to its collar. There, by the door," he gasped out.

Henry kept talking. Tommy kept rolling and giggling with the dog. Maguire sank down on the step, and opened the folded envelope. Inside was an extensive vet history on the dog, and a short, personal note.

> Her name is Taffy. She's almost four. The man who owned her was a pilot, so she's used to traveling—by plane, or car or any other way. Her owner died of cancer. She has no one else. She's extremely well trained. She just needs someone to love.
>
> You told me to go after what I wanted, Maguire. So that's what I'm doing. What I want... is for you to let this dog love you.

Maguire was still holding the note when the dog's golden head poked under his arm. She angled next to his side, sat down and put her head on his knee, closed her eyes. "Taffy," he said.

She wagged her tail faster than thunder, but her eyes stayed closed.

Maguire looked up at Tommy, at Henry.

"No one just gives someone else a dog. It's wrong at every level."

"I concur, sir."

"Think of the dog hair. The dirt. The drool. The difficulties traveling around with a dog. It's all horrendous."

"I was thinking the same thing, sir."

"I've never had a dog." Maguire sucked in a breath, let his fingers drift into the dog's thick fur. "I've had everything money could buy. I just never…had a dog. She couldn't possibly know that. I never said I wanted a dog."

"I never heard you say that," Henry agreed.

"Because I didn't. When I was a kid…nothing was steady. Great schools, everything a kid could want playwise. But moms didn't stick, not my original, or any of my father's replacements. We were always moving to different places, different cities. I got it."

"You got what, sir?"

"That that's the way it was. You have to be careful not to count on things. Because nothing stays the same. Material things, those you can always have. But things that live and breathe, Henry. It's just a lot easier not to get attached."

"Please, Mr. Cochran. Tell me we're not keeping her. Think of the dog hair. You might be allergic," Henry said hopefully. "In the summer, she could have fleas. She'll have to be brushed. You don't have time for something like a dog, sir."

"I can't believe she would do this to me."

"Neither can I, sir."

"Have you ever seen me duck a responsibility? Ever? Even once, Henry?"

"Never, sir."

"But I don't take in dogs. Or cats. Or people. Not

long term. You get attached. Then when something dies or leaves or divorces or whatever, your world's ripped out from under you. Asking for that is stupid. It's like napping on a train track."

Tommy was looking at him with a world of hope in his eyes; Henry was giving him the frantic say-no stare. Maguire's gaze narrowed on the dog.

This time, Carolina had gone over the line. Way, way, way over the line. She knew why a person drew lines in the sand. She knew about boundaries. She knew why a person needed boundaries—to be safe.

By throwing out those boundaries, Carolina knew perfectly well what she'd done.

She wasn't asking to be safe. Not anymore. Not from him.

Just take a breath, Carolina told herself. So she was terrified. Nothing new about that. She was a born wuss, for Pete's sake.

Maguire had taught her to dive off the deep end and not look back. And she'd been trying hard to live that way. Running some risks, making some changes, standing up. But Maguire wasn't here.

And her old wuss personality flaw had shown up big-time for this meeting.

She didn't belong here. The conference room was upstairs, located in the Department of Education, in downtown Indianapolis.

Naturally, she'd gotten lost just trying to find the place. The streets all had state names, like Vermont and New York and Washington. Only, she'd been looking for Ohio.

Being here was partly her own fault, she had to admit. She'd initiated the call to the State Board of Education. But after that, fate or kismet or coincidence or something had just kicked in on her. She managed to reach the state superintendent just by luck. By chance, the superintendent had a special ed child and could especially relate to Carolina. And it was pure luck that there was a conference scheduled on Dynamic New Ideas for Special Ed Children that week.

Carolina had just planned to dip a toe in, put out a few feelers. She never expected to be thrown off the deep end—which was what she called having to stand up in front of a microphone after lunch.

"I just met this young woman a few days ago," the superintendent said as he introduced her. "This is exactly what we've been talking about—finding someone to spearhead new directions in our special education program. We need someone to harness all the varied opinions from teachers, parents, administrators and doctors. To establish goals we all share, goals that are achievable, goals we can sink our teeth into. Carolina. Take it away!"

She didn't want to "take it away." She wanted to

curl up on a couch and disappear under a blanket. That not being an option, she strode to the podium in her red shoes and just…started.

The terror didn't leave her. But once she got going, her enthusiasm for the subject eased the public-speaking fears. People in the audience started nodding. She clearly wasn't the only one who had these ideas, who wanted to see change.

"We all know there's a disconnect between the people who spend time every day with special ed children—parents and teachers—and the people who have considerable power over their lives and choices. Doctors. Insurance people. Administrators. Teachers and parents are in a far better position to evaluate a child's potential than someone who only sees these kids for minutes at a time. We need the medical and health expertise—but we need a symposium where we can exchange information, about how things really are with these children. From new techniques to curriculum changes, we could do so much more…"

Heaven knew where all that passion came from, when she'd always been far more of a backseat driver than an instigator. Maybe it was Maguire's influence, who'd put the concept in her head that you have the right to love how you live.

He'd made her believe it somehow—that she could do anything. Even the things she was afraid of. If she just risked it all and put herself out there.

And as if her heart could do magician's tricks… suddenly, there he was. Her Maguire. Wearing slacks and a heavy cream-colored sweater, standing at the back of the long conference room. With a dog.

Dogs, of course, were forbidden in the building, but she knew Maguire's philosophy about that sort of thing. Show him any rule and he'd find an excuse to bend it.

Her voice faltered. Then speeded up. She kept talking, although she wasn't sure what she said. For darn sure, she had no idea what provoked them all to start applauding. The instant the superintendent stood up, Carolina was free to leave the podium and fly across the room.

"Hey, we didn't want to interrupt you. We can wait," Maguire said, but that's not what he communicated with his eyes.

She searched his face, still not certain why he was here. But then she just grabbed his arm. Outside the conference room, the hallway had occasional passersby. Someone dropped a file; two people ambled past deep in conversation—but it was quiet enough.

He leaned against the wall, looked at her as if all he wanted to do was look. And look. And look. For as long as there were stars.

Because Maguire wasn't a sentimental man, she warned herself not to hope too much. Maybe she was the one seeing those love stars. She tried to get a grip.

"How are you, my darling?" The croon wasn't for him, but for the dog. "You remember me, don't you? I told you we'd find a sucker to take you in, didn't I?"

"Are you calling me a sucker, Carolina?"

"Not often. Not much. But occasionally." She straightened, cocked her head. "Like that old song, I think you're one of those people who need somebody to love. And in the meantime…how on earth do you happen to be here?"

"As we both know, money doesn't buy everything—but it'll usually buy any information I want. Instead, I've been pretty much combing the universe to find you. I didn't have any clue that you'd be in Indianapolis, much less in the State Department of Education building."

"Well, believe me, neither did I. It's your fault." She leaned against the wall, too. Inches from his face. Inches from his mouth and eyes and the touch of him.

"My fault?"

"Yeah. I've been flunking a few of the lessons you taught me. I admit it. I couldn't always hold the line. My sister especially got to me. But my brother now, there, I was tough. You'd have been proud. Honest."

"Maybe I'm already proud, Carolina."

She wasn't going to cry, not in a public building. She wasn't even sure why they were still *in* the darned building, except that she didn't want to move an inch. Didn't want to be separated from that look in his eyes for even a millisecond.

"Sending me the shoe catalog was cruel."

"You sent me a dog, and you call *me* cruel? But I loved watching you and the shoe thing. It kept coming to me. When you love, you *love,* Carolina. All or nothing. All the way. Even when it hurts. I was afraid I'd never be able to offer you the same."

"You're out of your mind, as usual, Maguire. You have more love in you than any fifty other people."

"I never thought that. I don't know how you thought that. Why'd you send the tree-house books?"

"What makes you think *I* sent them? Did you like the one with the solar-heated shower?"

"Why'd you send them?" he repeated carefully.

She stopped scrubbing the dog's ears. "Because, Maguire, as cute as you are, you're not all that bright. You need to love how you live. You have all these places, but you don't have a home. A place where you feel safe. A place where you can put your feet up and just be yourself. A place where you don't have to do a single thing but enjoy the sunshine and the moonbeams."

"Carolina, quit with the silly talk. I need you to get serious."

She swallowed. "Okay. I'm serious."

"How are we going to get the dog in the tree house?"

"A sling. I almost sent you a catalog for those, too."

"All right. So the dog's solvable. But now comes the serious, critical problem. How am I going to get you in a tree house with me?"

She gulped. "I didn't know you wanted me in the tree house with you."

"I do. I want you in my life. Anywhere, anyhow I can get you. It's about falling that hard in love with you, Carolina. I never planned on it. It wasn't supposed to happen. Only now it has. And I'm afraid I'm stuck with wanting you, needing you, loving you, for the rest of my life."

"A definite problem," she concurred, and only then was aware that he'd taken her hands. Both of them. That he was holding both as if he was refusing to let go of a lifeline. "Well, here's the thing, Maguire. I need you to know…that I don't need a protector. Or a mentor. Or someone to keep me out of trouble. I did, I admit it. But not now."

"You're tough," Maguire concurred.

"It's been a journey. First to identify what really matters to me. And then to risk it all, no holds barred, to get what I want in my life. And that's love, Maguire. That's all I ever wanted from you."

He pulled her into his arms…and she pulled him into hers. Probably it was impossible to tell the difference. It was right, that's all she knew. The taste of him, the texture of his mouth, the way he turned a kiss into something thrilling and unforgettable, something more wondrous than she'd ever dreamed of. She tasted their future in that kiss.

"Maguire?" When they both broke for breath, they also instinctively aimed for the door. The sooner they were out of there and in a private place—with the dog, of course—the better.

"I was thinking that we could still get a marriage license this afternoon," he said.

"I was thinking that you'd better have money. Because I'm very likely going to give all mine away."

"I figured that. Right after I met you." Another kiss, this time on her brow, fast and possessive, just before he pushed the door open and the three of them hurried outside. "Let's go make a life, loved one. Our life. Our way."

* * * * *

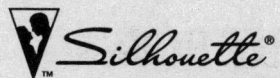 Silhouette®

COMING NEXT MONTH
Available November 30, 2010

#2083 A THUNDER CANYON CHRISTMAS
RaeAnne Thayne
Montana Mavericks: Thunder Canyon Cowboys

#2084 UNWRAPPING THE PLAYBOY
Marie Ferrarella
Matchmaking Mamas

#2085 THE BACHELOR'S CHRISTMAS BRIDE
Victoria Pade
Northbridge Nuptials

#2086 ONCE UPON A CHRISTMAS EVE
Christine Flynn
The Hunt for Cinderella

#2087 TWINS UNDER HIS TREE
Karen Rose Smith
The Baby Experts

#2088 THE CHRISTMAS PROPOSITION
Cindy Kirk
Rx for Love

REQUEST YOUR FREE BOOKS!
2 FREE NOVELS PLUS 2 FREE GIFTS!

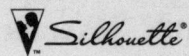

SPECIAL EDITION
Life, Love and Family!

YES! Please send me 2 FREE Silhouette® Special Edition® novels and my 2 FREE gifts (gifts are worth about $10). After receiving them, if I don't wish to receive any more books, I can return the shipping statement marked "cancel." If I don't cancel, I will receive 6 brand-new novels every month and be billed just $4.24 per book in the U.S. or $4.99 per book in Canada. That's a saving of 15% off the cover price! It's quite a bargain! Shipping and handling is just 50¢ per book.* I understand that accepting the 2 free books and gifts places me under no obligation to buy anything. I can always return a shipment and cancel at any time. Even if I never buy another book from Silhouette, the two free books and gifts are mine to keep forever.

235/335 SDN E5RG

Name	(PLEASE PRINT)	
Address		Apt. #
City	State/Prov.	Zip/Postal Code

Signature (if under 18, a parent or guardian must sign)

Mail to the **Silhouette Reader Service:**
IN U.S.A.: P.O. Box 1867, Buffalo, NY 14240-1867
IN CANADA: P.O. Box 609, Fort Erie, Ontario L2A 5X3

Not valid for current subscribers to Silhouette Special Edition books.

Want to try two free books from another line?
Call 1-800-873-8635 or visit www.morefreebooks.com.

* Terms and prices subject to change without notice. Prices do not include applicable taxes. N.Y. residents add applicable sales tax. Canadian residents will be charged applicable provincial taxes and GST. Offer not valid in Quebec. This offer is limited to one order per household. All orders subject to approval. Credit or debit balances in a customer's account(s) may be offset by any other outstanding balance owed by or to the customer. Please allow 4 to 6 weeks for delivery. Offer available while quantities last.

Your Privacy: Silhouette is committed to protecting your privacy. Our Privacy Policy is available online at www.eHarlequin.com or upon request from the Reader Service. From time to time we make our lists of customers available to reputable third parties who may have a product or service of interest to you. If you would prefer we not share your name and address, please check here. ☐

Help us get it right—We strive for accurate, respectful and relevant communications. To clarify or modify your communication preferences, visit us at www.ReaderService.com/consumerschoice.

SSE10R

Spotlight on
Classic

Quintessential, modern love stories
that are romance at its finest.

See the next page
to enjoy a sneak peek from
the Harlequin® Romance series.

*See below for a sneak peek from our classic
Harlequin® Romance® line.*

Introducing DADDY BY CHRISTMAS by Patricia Thayer.

MIA caught sight of Jarrett when he walked into the open lobby. It was hard not to notice the man. In a charcoal business suit with a crisp white shirt and striped tie covered by a dark trench coat, he looked more Wall Street than small-town Colorado.

Mia couldn't blame him for keeping his distance. He was probably tired of taking care of her.

Besides, why would a man like Jarrett McKane be interested in her? Why would he want to take on a woman expecting a baby? Yet he'd done so many things for her. He'd been there when she'd needed him most. How could she not care about a man like that?

Heart pounding in her ears, she walked up behind him. Jarrett turned to face her. "Did you get enough sleep last night?"

"Yes, thanks to you," she said, wondering if he'd thought about their kiss. Her gaze went to his mouth, then she quickly glanced away. "And thank you for not bringing up my meltdown."

Jarrett couldn't stop looking at Mia. Blue was definitely her color, bringing out the richness of her eyes.

"What meltdown?" he said, trying hard to focus on what she was saying. "You were just exhausted from lack of sleep and worried about your baby."

He couldn't help remembering how, during the night, he'd kept going in to watch her sleep. How strange was that? "I hope you got enough rest."

She nodded. "Plenty. And you're a good neighbor for

coming to my rescue."

He tensed. Neighbor? *What neighbor kisses you like I did?* "That's me, just the full-service landlord," he said, trying to keep the sarcasm out of his voice. He started to leave, but she put her hand on his arm.

"Jarrett, what I meant was you went beyond helping me." Her eyes searched his face. "I've asked far too much of you."

"Did you hear me complain?"

She shook her head. "You should. I feel like I've taken advantage."

"Like I said, I haven't minded."

"And I'm grateful for everything…"

Grasping her hand on his arm, Jarrett leaned forward. The memory of last night's kiss had him aching for another. "I didn't do it for your gratitude, Mia."

Gorgeous tycoon Jarrett McKane has never believed in Christmas—but he can't help being drawn to soon-to-be-mom Mia Saunders! Christmases past were spent alone…and now Jarrett may just have a fairy-tale ending for all his Christmases future!

Available December 2010, only from Harlequin® Romance®.

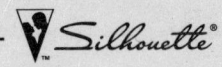

SPECIAL EDITION

USA TODAY BESTSELLING AUTHOR

MARIE FERRARELLA

**BRINGS YOU ANOTHER
HEARTWARMING STORY FROM**

When Lilli McCall disappeared on him
after he proposed, Kullen Manetti swore
never to fall in love again. Eight years later
Lilli is back in his life, threatening to break
down all the walls he's put up to
safeguard his heart.

UNWRAPPING
THE PLAYBOY

*Available December
wherever books are sold.*

Visit Silhouette Books at www.eHarlequin.com

SSE65566R